懋典文化

Workplace

職場English

Business Communication
Skills Training

英文王

會話能力進階手冊

商務英語 常見用法 附贈

張文娟 著

國家圖書館出版品預行編目資料

職場英文王：會話能力進階手冊 / 張文娟著.
-- 初版. -- 新北市：雅典文化, 民106. 07
　　面；　公分. --（英語工具書；14）
ISBN 978-986-5753-84-9（18K平裝附光碟片）
1. 商業英文　　2. 會話
805. 188　　　　　　　　　106007747

英語工具書系列　14

職場英文王：會話能力進階手冊

著／張文娟

責任編輯／張文娟

內文排版／王國卿

封面設計／姚恩涵

法律顧問：方圓法律事務所／涂成樞律師

總經銷：永續圖書有限公司
永續圖書線上購物網
www.foreverbooks.com.tw

CVS代理／美璟文化有限公司
TEL：（02）2723-9968
FAX：（02）2723-9668

出版日／2017年7月

雅典文化

出版社　22103　新北市汐止區大同路三段194號9樓之1
TEL　（02）8647-3663
FAX　（02）8647-3660

序 言

　　自從網路時代來臨，世界各地皆快速國際化，英語早已成為最重要的國際溝通語言，也是大多數企業招募新進員工的基本要求，因此如何將自己的英文提升至心儀公司要求的標準之上，特別是英語口說的表達能力，成為所有求職者都必須面對的課題。

　　本書的目的就是想幫助讀者加強商務英語的會話能力，提綱挈領的主題式編寫方向，有助於提高學習效率，如果能夠靈活運用書中的常用表達方式，反覆聆聽 MP3 音檔的錄音，讓所聽到的示範例句深植於腦海中，那麼當遇到臨時需要派上用場的時候，便能不假思索，不費吹灰之力，自動在腦中搜尋出合宜的英語表達方式，讓對方或雇主留下深刻印象。

　　英語只是談生意的工具，最重要還是在於達成任務。筆者於書中儘量選用基礎且常用的英文字彙與片語，想要強調的是，不需要用到過於艱深的英文，仍然還是可以順利談成生意。當然，不同程度的讀者可以視其程度與場合需要，自由變化書中內容，要點在於靈活運用，也因此本書所適合的讀者群非常之廣。

　　筆者才疏學淺，書中內容如有需要更正之處，還望大家不吝指教，只希望這本書可以發揮拋磚引玉之效，對需要用到英語的商務人士真能有所助益。

　　本書校閱承文家楹小姐與高惠治先生幫忙，謹此誌謝。

張文娟

2017 年二月

Chapter 1.

Good Answers to Interview
回答面試官 010

Chapter 2.

New Employee Orientation
新進員工訓練 062

Chapter 3.

Telephoning
電話用語 074

Chapter 4.

Presentation
簡報 088

Chapter 5.

On a Business Trip
出差 100

Chapter 6.

Touring a Trade Fair
參觀商展 116

Chapter 7.

Discrimination in the Workplace
職場上的歧視 126

Chapter 8.

Negotiation
協商 138

Chapter 9.

Formal Business Meeting
正式商務會議 152

Chapter 10.

Signing a Contract
簽訂合約 164

Chapter 11.

Sales Language
銷售用語 176

Chapter 12.

Payment Terms
付款方式 188

Chapter 13.

Packing, Shipment & Insurance
包裝、裝運及保險 196

Chapter
14.

Claim & Arbitration
索賠及仲裁 206

Chapter
15.

Agency
代理 216

Chapter
16.

Customer Service
客戶服務 226

Chapter
17.

Collaboration Across Departments
跨部門合作 242

Chapter
18.

Hosting a Guest
接待訪客 254

Chapter
19.

Arranging Travel Plans
安排旅遊計畫 268

Chapter
20.

Annual Self-Evaluation
年度自我評量 278

附錄
1

Letter of Application
求職信 292

附錄
2

Resume
履歷表 302

附錄
3

Autobiography
自傳 314

Chapter 1

Good Answers to Interview

回答面試官

一、簡介 Short Introduction

　　面試是進入心儀公司的決定關鍵，而就企業而言，面試官最想要知道的就是，層層篩選後進入面試的候選人，是否真的像履歷表上所描述的那麼理想，以及如何用最短的時間挑選出最合適的人選。無論是否爲外商，英語面試早已成爲人才招募不可或缺的一環，所以想要從中脫穎而出，務必要做好充足準備，本章所提供的常見情境問題，可以幫助讀者於腦中預先演練，請先比較新手欠缺經驗的回答，然後再參考本書建議的答法，研擬出適合自己的說法，並且用英語來表達。只要面試前不斷設想可能預見的問題，再設法模擬回答，到了面試現場就算是遇到了完全沒想過的問題，也因爲平時的練習，反應速度就會增快不少。

二、常用表達方式 Useful Expressions

 01

這該怎麼答？

1 What are your greatest strengths?
你的最大優點為何？

新手

① Do not pay attention to the job's requirements.
不注意看工作要求為何。

例 "I am especially good at writing fictions, and that's why when I heard there was a vacant position of the copyrights director in your publishing house, I immediately applied."

「我特別擅長寫小說，所以我一聽說你們出版社有版權主任的職缺，便馬上提出申請。」

② Boast too much.　　　太自誇。

例 "My greatest strength is not having any weaknesses."

「我最大的優點便是沒有缺點。」

③ Too humble.　　　太謙虛。

例 "Let me think about it.... I think I still have to improve myself much to fit in well with your company."
「讓我想想看……我想我還要多改善自己才能適合在貴公司工作。」

建議

①Answers should be about the job's requirements.
答案應該要與工作要求相關。

例 "I am particularly good at organizing details and negotiating with English native speakers. With two years of experience of working in a copyright agency in the past, I am sure I am the best person for this position of the copyrights director."
「我特別擅長安排細節項目還有與英語母語人士協商，過去我曾經在版權代理公司工作過兩年，因此我相信自己為版權主任一職的最佳人選。」

②Give good examples to support statements.
舉出具體例子來作證論點。

例 "Above all, I think in terms of the employer and have made a very positive contribution to the whole company. In the past year, I successfully hosted visitors from Shanghai and organized a company trip to Tokyo. Not only that, I managed to reduce the costs of new staff training by 50%."

「最重要的是，我為以雇主立場來考量，對公司整體都做出非常正面的貢獻。過去一年下來，我成功接待了上海來的訪客，妥當安排好公司的東京之旅，除此之外，經過我的努力，新進員工訓練的費用得以省下一半。」

③ Give good comments from others.
舉出他人的好評。

例 "My former boss thinks that I helped him solve many problems. It must be because I always think in the shoes of the employer."

「我上個老闆認為我幫他解決了很多問題，這一定是因為我總是站在雇主的角度來思考。」

Unit 2 What are your greatest weaknesses? 02

你的最大缺點為何？

新手

①Show serious weaknesses.
暴露出嚴重缺點。

例 "To be honest, I don't have any weaknesses, except that sometimes I have no number sense. Quite often I do not catch Arabic numerals in English listening."

「老實說，我沒有什麼缺點，除了有時候沒有數字概念，我常常在聽英文的時候，沒掌握到阿拉伯數字。」

②Not to the point of the interview.
與面談不相關。

例 "Whenever I see sweets, I just can't help eating too much."

「每次我看到甜點都會失控而吃太多。」

③Not sincere.　　　　　　不誠懇。

例 "My greatest weakness is not having any weaknesses because I am a perfectionist."

「我最大的缺點便是沒有缺點，因為我是個完美主義者。」

① **Positive statements.**
正面的說法。

例 "We all have weaknesses. If I have to name one of my weaknesses, it would be often putting much more efforts into the job than needed to achieve the best end result. Sometimes it would bother the other people in the same team."

「每個人都有缺點，如果一定要我舉出我的一項缺點的話，那就是我經常會為了達到最佳成效而投入更多的心血，這點有時候會讓同團隊的人感到困擾。」

② **Be sincere and show willingness to improve.**
誠懇地表示願意改善。

例 "Math has never been my strong point. If this job has to deal with numbers, I will always carry a calculator with me and do my best to work with numbers."

「數學一直不是我的強項，如果這份工作要處理數字的話，我會隨時攜帶計算機，盡全力處理數字。」

③ **Give an example.**　　　　提出一個例子。

例　"Usually I never miss a deadline, but in the last job, in order to have the best quality of work, I was once a week late to hand in my assignment. Occasionally, I revise the work several times in order to get the best result."

「通常我不會有遲交的情形，但是在上份工作中，有一次我為了要達到最佳工作成果，遲了一星期才交件。有時候，我會為了要得到最好的結果而修改很多次。」

Unit

3 **Why did you leave your last company?**

MP3 03

你為什麼離開上一家公司？

新手

① Blame it all on others.
將過錯全都推給別人。

例 "My former boss is a bully. He always picked on me and was never happy about whatever I did so I quit."

「我上一個老闆會霸凌人，他老愛挑我的毛病，對我所做的任何工作從不滿意，所以我辭職了。」

② Do not show yourself in a positive light.
沒有展現正面的形象。

例 "I was fired."

「我被炒魷魚了。」

③ Show you are not easy to work with.
表現出難以共事的樣子。

例 "Whenever I had problems I had to ask someone, there was nobody there to support me. All the people in the office gave me all the tough work and took away all my credits."

「每當我有問題要請教人時，那裡沒有人可以給我任何支持，辦公室裡所有的人都要我做苦工，還拿走我的所有功勞。」

① **Provide reasonable explanations.**
   提供合理的解釋。

 "My former boss did not quite agree with me on some ways I handled my assignments. In the job description of your job offer, I can see that my style of management fits in with your company. That is why I wanted to apply for the job."

「我上一個老闆對於我的一些工作方式有不同意見，從你們的工作描述看來，我認為我的管理風格與你們公司相符合，因此我想要申請這份工作。」

② **Give reasons you cannot control.**
   提供你無法控制的原因。

 "My boss of the previous company decided to set a stop-loss point and closed his business."

「我上一個公司的老闆決定設一個停損點，結束營業。」

③Show willingness to learn from the past.
表現願意從過去經驗學習。

例 "Just like everyone else, I made a few mistakes at work, and I took the responsibility by leaving the company. I am sure I would learn from my own mistakes and would never repeat them in my new job."

「就像所有人一樣，我在工作時犯了些錯誤，我離開公司以示負責，我非常確信可以從自己的錯誤中學習，絕不會在新工作中重蹈覆轍。」

Unit 4 What did you like and dislike about your last job?

MP3 04

對於上一份工作，你最喜歡和最不喜歡的部分為何？

① Not specific enough.

不夠詳細。

例 "I liked to have make-up holidays, and I hated overwork."

「我喜歡補假，痛恨加班。」

② Give no credits to the previous employer at all.
完全不讚許舊老闆。

例 "Our former supervisor had absolute no ideas what we were up to and did not seem to care. Whenever we reported our problems with the clients to him, he showed little interest to listen to us. Nobody wants to work for such a person."

「我們的前主管從來都不知道我們在做什麼，而且他似乎一點也不在乎，無論我們什麼時候向他報告客戶的問題，他都不想聽，沒有人喜歡為這樣的人工作。」

③ Not aware that the new company has the same problems, too.
不清楚新公司也有相同問題。

例 "What I really disliked about my previous job is that we had a system of job responsibility. I often got calls from my supervisor after work hours. Last week I was asked to make calls to the clients in the States at 9 pm, I decided to quit."

「在上份工作中，我最不喜歡的就是責任制，我經常會於下班時間接到我主管的電話。上星期他們要求我在晚上九點打電話給美國的客戶的時候，我便決定辭職。」

建議

① Provide detailed explanations.
提供詳細的解釋。

例 "What I liked most in my previous company is that we could apply for make-up holidays when we had a good reason, such as going abroad to attend trade shows. What bothered me most was working over-time even when there was really no need to. Most employees would feel highly pressured if they had left the office earlier than the former boss."

「我最喜歡上一個公司的是可以申請補假，只要我們有像是出國參展那樣的正當理由；最讓我不高興的是不必要的加班，大部分的員工如果比老闆先離開辦公室，便會倍感壓力。」

---

②Do some research and compare the new company with the previous one.
做點研究，比較新舊公司。

例 "In my previous work, I was in charge of marketing and I liked my job. The progress was, however, quite slow because I was the only person taking care of the job. In your company, you have a well-trained team to do marketing research. That's why I think it is a better place for me to work in."

「在我上一份工作中，我負責行銷而且我喜歡我的工作，但是進展頗緩慢，因為我是唯一負責這個工作的人。你們公司有訓練有素的團隊負責行銷研究工作，因此我認為這是對我較佳的工作地方。」

---

③Do your homework and compare the new boss with the former one.
做足功課，比較新舊老闆。

例 "My previous company offered me a good staff training program, but my supervisor at that time always likes micromanaging everything in the office. As a team leader I really disliked it. Many people say your boss trust employees very much and encourage them to develop their own ways of solving problems. That's the main reason I would like to work for this company."

「我上個公司提供了我良好的員工訓練計劃，但是我那時候的上司總是喜歡管任何微不足道的小事，作為團隊的領導者我真的很不喜歡這一點；很多人說你們的老闆非常信任員工，並且鼓勵他們研發自己解決問題的方式，這就是我想要在這家公司效力的主要原因。」

Unit

5 Please tell me about your biggest achievement so far.

MP3 05

請告訴我你至今最大的工作成就？

新手

① Too minor, not impressive enough.

太微小，不夠讓人留下深刻印象。

 "My biggest achievement would be never taking sick leave so far."

「我最大的成就是從來沒有請過病假。」

② Not special enough.　　不夠特別。

 "I have never missed any deadline so far."

「到目前為止我從來沒有錯過任何的最後期限。」

③ Boast too much.　　太自誇。

 "The thing is that I've had so many outstanding achievements so far that I wouldn't be able to tell you which ones are the biggest."

「問題是我至今有如此多過人的成就，以致於我無法告訴你我最大的工作成就為何。」

建議

① Provide a specific example.
舉出特別的例子。

例 " There was that one time we had to work against a deadline, and I led my team to pull through and delivered a great performance in the end. Not only that, I managed to organize a press conference at the last minute, and the response of the audience was fantastic. Everyone in the company was really impressed by my capabilities of working under pressure."

「有一次我們必須要趕在最後期限前完工，我帶領我的團隊排除萬難，最後表現非常傑出，不只這樣，我還在最後一刻安排了記者會，觀眾反應極佳，我在壓力下能有這樣優秀的表現，公司裡的每個人都對此留下深刻印象。」

② Answers should be about the job's requirements.
答案須與工作要求相關。

例 "In my last job, I worked in the sales department in a real estate agency and won a special award in the company. My social skills and natural talents in finding clients helped me achieve the best sales performance. To sum up, I am very confident to take up the job as a sales manager in your company."

「上一份工作中，我在一家房地產公司的業務部服務，獲得了公司內的特殊成就獎，我的社交能力與發掘客戶的天份使我達成了最佳銷售成績。總而言之，我非常有信心擔任你們公司業務經理一職。」

---

③ **Tell about recognitions from your previous supervisors and coworkers.**
提及過去上司與同事的肯定。

例 "My biggest achievements so far would be being a natural leader in the office. All previous supervisors and coworkers found me trustworthy and often approached me with their problems. I might not be the most capable person in the company, but I was always regarded as the most likable person."

「我最大的成就是總會自然而然地成為辦公室的領導人物，所有從前的上司與同事都覺得我非常值得信賴，經常請教我他們的問題。或許我並非公司裡最有能力的人，但是我總是被視為最令人喜愛的人。」

Unit

6 **Why have you changed jobs so frequently?**

MP3 06

你為何這麼常換工作？

新手

① Do not take responsibility.
不負責任。

例 "The employers I've had are to blame for this."
「這都要怪我從前的雇主。」

② Do not admit it. 不承認這一點。

例 "Young people at my age have changed their jobs much more often than I do. So far I've only changed jobs ten times within three years. It is not too bad."
「像我這種年齡的年輕人通常都比我還更常換工作，到目前為止我只不過在三年內換過十份工作，不算太糟。」

③ Make the interviewer afraid you might change your job again soon.
使面試官擔心你很快又會換工作。

例 "Whoever offers me a better pay, I would work there. Who wouldn't do that, right?"
「誰付給我的薪水高，我就會到那邊工作，每個人都會這麼做，對吧？」

①Provide information about your career history.
提供關於你的工作經歷的資訊。

例 "When I just entered the job market, I was not sure what I could do so I tried many jobs. That's why I have more experiences than most people at my age. Most of the jobs I have had were in the banking industry, and I was with my last company quite a long time. Unfortunately the company went bankrupt, and that's why now I'd like to find a new company to contribute what I have learned before to."

「我剛開始進入就業市場時，並不太清楚我能夠做什麼，所以我嘗試了很多工作，因此我比同年齡的人所擁有的經驗來得多。我大多都在銀行業工作，而且我待在上一個公司有很長的一段時間，很不幸的是那家公司倒閉了，因此現在我想要找一家新公司來貢獻我從前學到的一切。」

②Give reasons you could not control.
提供你無法控制的原因。

例 "Tough economy has made my previous companies downsize the employees. In the meantime, in order to pay for my mortgage, I had no time to look for a suitable job and had to accept any offers I could get. That's why I have had to change job more frequently than others. Right now, I am very willing to work for your company on a long-term basis."

「我之前的公司曾因為經濟問題而裁員，在這當中，我為了要付房貸，沒有時間找合適的工作，只好接受任何可以得到的工作，這就是我比其他人還常換工作的原因。現在，我非常願意為你們公司長期服務。」

③Promise you will be a stable worker.
保證你會穩定工作。

例 "When I graduated from the university, I went on working holidays in Australia because of my love for traveling. Afterwards, I went to New Zealand and worked part-time there for a couple of years. Now the travel bug is gone and I'd really like to settle down in Taipei. If you could give me the opportunity to work here, you'll see how much my language and other skills can contribute to your company."

「大學畢業後我因為熱愛旅行而到澳洲打工度假，之後我到紐西蘭兼差有一兩年。現在的我已經不再那麼熱衷旅遊，非常想要在台北安頓下來，如果你願意給我機會於此工作，就會發現我的語言與其它技能可以對貴公司做出極大的貢獻。」

Unit 7 How do you deal with stress?

MP3 07

你如何處理壓力？

 新手

① Not enough information.
資訊不足。

例 "I can handle stress better than others."
「我有過人的抗壓力。」

② Too humble, do not show much confidence.
太謙虛，顯得很沒自信。

例 "Right now I am still learning how to cope with stress."
「我現在還在學習如何抗壓。」

③ Self-flattery.　　　　　自我感覺太好。

例 "Stress? I seldom have stress because of my outstanding working skills."
「壓力？我很少有壓力，因為我的工作能力超強。」

建議

① Give an affirmative reply and tell about one good example.

正面回答，並且提供一個好例子。

例 "Usually I can manage stress pretty well and work well under reasonable pressure. Once our clients changed his appointment at short notice, and as a result, I had to lead our team to work against an earlier deadline. My previous boss was amazed at my calmness to cope with stress."

「通常我很能管理壓力，並且能在適度壓力下有良好的工作表現，有一次我們客戶臨時改變會談時間，導致我必須帶領我們團隊趕在最後期限前提早交件，我上一位老闆非常訝異，我處理壓力時能如此冷靜。」

② Provide positive answers.

提供正面答案。

例 "It's a stressful world we are living in, and we all have to develop ways of coping with stress. I believe that one can have the best performance under the right amount of stress. That's why usually I regard pressure at work as positive stress. Some of my common ways of relieving stress are meeting up with friends, taking exercise and riding a bike in the countryside."

「我們處在一個充滿壓力的世界，因此每個人都要培養對抗壓力的方法，我認為一個人在適當壓力下會有最佳的表現，因此我經常將工作壓力視為正向的壓力。通常我紓解壓力的方法為和朋友聚會、運動、到郊外騎腳踏車。」

③ Show you are good but are willing to learn more about stress management.
表現你雖然很好，但是還想多學習如何管理壓力。

例 "In general, I could deal with stress at work well, but there is always room for improvement. Hopefully I can learn more about the capabilities of working under stress in the position in your company."

「通常我很會處理壓力，但總還是有改善的空間，希望我能在貴公司的這份職位上學習更多在壓力下工作的能力。」

Unit

8 Are you a good team player?

(MP3) 08

你在團隊中表現得如何？

新手

①Not assertive enough.

不夠肯定。

例 "I can get along with most people in a team"
「我可以與團隊中的大部分人保持良好的關係。」

新手

②Sound doubtful.

聽來讓人懷疑。

例 "I prefer to work alone, but if I have to, I can work in a team as well."

「我比較喜歡獨自工作，不過如果必要的話，我也可以在團隊工作。」

③Signs the interviewer might worry about.
面試官可能會煩惱的徵兆。

例 "In my previous company, everyone in the team liked to work with me, but my former boss just wasn't satisfied with me at all."

「在我上個公司中，團隊中的每個人都喜歡與我工作，但是我的上個闆對我就是一點也不滿意。」

建議

① Focus on team spirit.
專注於團隊精神。

例 "All my former employers think I show great team spirit in whatever I do. Very often I would not care much about personal gain for the best performance of the team."

「所有我從前的雇主都認為，我無論做什麼都表現出優秀的團隊精神，我經常會為了追求團隊的最佳表現而不顧個人的利益。」

② Give an affirmative reply and cite references by former colleagues.
正面回答，提供舊同事的正面評價。

例 "Almost all my former colleagues regard me as a fantastic team player. Especially in the law firm I worked for last time, all of the coworkers I worked with asked me to stay because I had been such an exceptional team leader."

「幾乎所有我從前的同事認為我在團隊中表現傑出，特別是在我上次服務的律師事務所，所有與我共事過的同事都請我留下來，正是因為我的團隊領導能力極為不凡。」

③ Provide positive answers with examples.
提供正面答案，並且附上例子。

例 "Team work can produce the best work result, and I enjoy working in a team. Very often I would naturally become the team leader in a team because of my leadership skills. When our team went on the business trip in the States last time, I coordinated almost everything with little preparation. Everyone in the team was thankful for the work I put into, and I got a salary raise afterwards from my former boss."

「團體合作可以產生最佳的工作績效，我非常喜歡與團隊中的人共事。經常自然而然我就會因為領導力而成為團隊的領導者。上回我們團隊到美國出差時，我幾乎沒有什麼準備就安排了所有事項，團隊中的所有人都對我付出的努力而感恩，而且我上個老闆在那趟出差後為我加薪。」

Unit 9 Do you usually pay attention to detail very well?

🎧 MP3 09

通常你很能夠注意到細節嗎？

① Do not take the question seriously enough.
對問題的態度不夠嚴肅。

例 "Since I am applying for the sales manager, I think there should be a secretary to pay attention to detail for me, right?"

「既然我所申請的職位為業務經理，我想應該會有個秘書來為我注意細節吧。」

② Too vague, not affirmative enough.
太模糊，不夠肯定。

例 "I can deal with major issues very well; as to minor issues, I think I have to pay more attention to detail."

「我非常能夠處理大事，至於小事，我想我得要多注意細節。」

③ Not a satisfactory answer for most employers.
對大部分雇主來說並非是滿意答案。

例 "It all comes down to how much you care about in the issue. If it something is what I am really interested in, I would not have problems to pay attention to detail."

「追根究柢這要看你對這件事有多關心，如果這是一件我真正有興趣的事，就不會有注意細節的問題。」

建議

①Analytical approach to the assigned work.
分析所分派到的任務。

例 "I would say yes. Whenever I am assigned tasks, I always analyze the components of the work to detail."

「我想我很能注意到細節，每當我一接到任務，我總是將我的工作做細部分析。」

②Pay attention to detail and can therefore work efficiently.
因為注意細節而有效率。

例 "I can always work very efficiently because I pay special attention to detail. In this way, I can avoid many mistakes others often make."

「我工作總是極為有效率，因為我特別注意細節，如此一來，避免掉了不少別人常會犯的錯。」

③Cite references by important people
舉出重要人物的推薦。

例 "When I worked as a secretary in the East & West Trading Firm, my supervisor, Mr. Datong Huang, often praised me for my attention to detail. Later on, my skills to tackle small details had become better and better, and eventually I was given a high raise."

「我在東西貿易公司當祕書的時候，我的上司黃大同先生經常讚美我注意細節的能力，之後，我處理小細節的能力越來越好，最後我得到了高額加薪。」

Unit
10 **What have you learned from your previous jobs?**

你從之前的工作中學到了什麼？

新手

① Sounds full of yourself.
聽起來自信過度高。

例 "I knew this trade already very well before taking up my last job so I was always the one who taught my colleagues."

「在我開始上一份工作前，我對這一行已瞭若指掌，所以總是我在教我的同事們。」

② Sounds like you were very weak.
聽起來你曾經很脆弱。

例 "What I have learned from my previous job is never to trust others."

「我從之前的工作中學到了千萬不要相信別人。」

③ Do not care about the job's requirements.
不管工作要求為何。

例 "From my previous job I have learned how to use Word and Excel, and therefore I believe I can provide excellent customer service in your restaurant."

「我從之前的工作中學會了如何使用 Word 和 Excel，因此我相信我能夠在你們餐廳提供良好的客戶服務。」

建議

① Pay attention to the job's requirements.
注意工作要求。

例 "During the time I worked for my previous company, I had learned to manage my time well. I am sure I can apply this skill to the work of the event manager in your company."

「在前一個公司的工作期間，我學會了妥善管理時間，我確信可以將此技巧運用到貴公司活動經理這個職務上。」

② Demonstrate your high learning potential.
說明你的學習潛力之強。

例 "Once I was asked to learn to use Excel, and it only took me one week to master it. When it comes to learning new technology, my learning potential is unlimited."

「有一次公司要求我學 Excel，我只花了一星期就完全學會了，只要是學習新科技，我真的是潛力無窮。」

③Show your willingness to learn more.
展現你願意學習的誠意。

例 "Although I had learned a great deal from my previous job, such as media management, I am always happy to learn more to be a capable sales manager."

「雖然我從上一份工作中學到很多東西，例如媒體管理，但是我一直願意做更多的學習，好成為一個有能力的業務經理。」

11 Are you good at facing challenges?

新手

① Have reservations about it.
對此語帶保留。

例 "It really depends on what kind of challenges, right? As you might know, sometimes some employers really have very unreasonable expectations of their employees."

「這真的要看什麼樣的挑戰，對吧？或許你也知道，有時候有些雇主對員工的要求真的很不合理。」

② Reply negatively.　　負面回答。

例 "Usually I try to avoid too much stress. Employers should have reasonable expectations. It is really too much to ask a new secretary to face unreasonable challenges, isn't it?"

「通常我盡量避免過高的壓力，雇主的期待應該要合理，要是丟給一個新來的秘書不合理的挑戰，不是有些過分嗎？」

③ Not willing to challenge oneself.
不願自我挑戰。

 "The biggest challenge I've faced so far is heavy workload, and I have dealt with it pretty well. I am pretty content with my capabilities."

「我所面臨過的最大挑戰便是龐大的工作量，我還算處理得宜。就目前來說，我對我的能力非常滿意。」

建議

① Reply affirmatively.
肯定回答。

例 "Usually I get especially motivated when facing challenges. The greater the obstacle is, the more I want to overcome it."

「我通常在面對挑戰的時候特別能激勵自己；障礙越大，我就越想克服。」

② Show you are good at it.
表現出你在這方面很行。

例 "If there is no challenge, there will be no breakthrough. I am a person who constantly challenges himself. It is my belief that by pushing myself to achieve high goals, I can make great progress."

「如果沒有挑戰就不會有突破。我是個不斷自我挑戰的人，我相信藉由鞭策自己達成崇高目標，才能有大進步。」

③Tell about an example. 舉例說明。

例 "There was this time I was required to run a workshop about "English E-Mails", and it seemed like an impossible challenge to me. With very little experience of public speaking, I practiced the talk over and over before the workshop. In the end, both my supervisor and the new staff were very satisfied with my performance."

「有一次有人要求我主持關於英文電子郵件的工作坊，這對我來說似乎像是個不可能的挑戰，我的公眾演講經驗不足，所以我在工作坊之前不斷演練，最後，我的上司和新進員工都對我的表現很滿意。」

Unit
12 How do you go about solving
problems in your work?

MP3 12

新手

① **Not very flexible.**
很沒有彈性。

 "Most problems occurred before. That's why I always ask about standard ways in the company to handle them."
「大部分問題從前都發生過，所以我總是問公司的標準處理方法。」

② **Put off the problems.**　拖延問題。

 "Time is the best solution of most problems, and therefore I prefer to let the future take care of itself."
「時間是大部分問題的最佳解決辦法，因此我寧願讓未來自然發展。」

③ **Ignore the possible problems in the future.**
忽略未來可能的問題。

"Usually I seldom worry about how to prevent possible future problems because in the future, the time will be totally different anyway."

「通常我很少煩惱如何避免未來可能的問題，因為反正在將來會是完全不相同的時代。」

建議

① Analyze the problems.

分析問題。

 "When I face new and difficult problems, I always try to analyze them calmly and carefully. If I cannot find a solution, I would approach experts with better analytical skills to help me."

「我面對新的難題時，總會試著冷靜且仔細地分析問題，如果我沒有辦法找到解決辦法，便會找更能分析問題的專家來幫忙我。」

② Ask the right questions. 問正確的問題。

 "The key approach in solving problems is to ask the right questions, for example, what I should do to break the obstacles down and conquer them one by one."

「解決問題的最關鍵辦法就是問正確的問題，例如，我該要怎麼做才能將障礙分解開來，然後一一克服呢？」

③ Just do it!　　　　　　　做就對了！

例 "Very often it is not easy in the beginning to start to solve any problems. Once the approach is decided, all it takes is courage and determination to pull through all issues."

「通常一開始要解決任何問題都不太容易，一旦決定好了要採取什麼做法，再來只要有勇氣與決心就能貫徹解決所有問題。」

Unit

⑬ Don't you think you are overqualified for this job?　🎧 13

你難道不覺得這份工作對你來說是大材小用？

新手

① Say you'll only work here for a short time.
說你只願意短暫於此工作。

例 "I've got to start from somewhere, but as long as I find a better job, I'll let you know."

「我總得要找個地方開始吧，不過只要我找到更好的工作，就會讓你知道。」

② Ask for much better pay.　要求大幅提高待遇。

例 "Since we both think I would be overqualified for this job, why don't you offer me a better pay?"

「既然我們都認為這份工作對我來說是大材小用，那你何不提個高一點的待遇？」

③ Turn down this job offer.　拒絕此份工作。

例 "To be honest, I also think I am too overqualified for this job. Well, maybe you should look for someone else to fill this position."

「老實說，我也覺得這份工作對我來說太過於大材小用，那麼，或許你們該找別人來填補這個職缺。」

①Thanks for the compliment.
謝謝對方的讚美。

例 "Thank you for your compliment to my skills and accomplishments. Hopefully, I can have the opportunity to polish my skills and make contribution to your company."

「謝謝對我技能與成就的讚美，希望我能有機會更加磨練我的技能，對貴公司做出貢獻。」

②Pay compliments to the company you want to enter.
讚美想進入的公司。

例 "Your great reputation makes me want to work here. In the travel industry, your company is regarded as the leading one, and it would be an honor for me to become a member of the tour guides in this renowned travel agency."

「你們優良的聲譽讓我想要在這裡工作，貴公司被視作旅遊業界的箇中翹楚，如果能成為這家著名的旅行社的導遊之一，我會感到很光榮。」

③ This job fits in with my career plan.
這份工作符合我的生涯規劃。

例 "At this stage of my life, this job actually fits perfectly in with my long-term career plan. I believe one can learn most from working in a small company."

「在現階段,這份工作事實上非常符合我的長程生涯規劃,我認為在小公司工作能學到最多的東西。」

Unit 14 MP3 14

Where do you see yourself in five years?

你預見五年後的自己會是如何？

新手

① Not clear, too vague.
不清楚，太模糊。

例 "In five years? I can't even see myself in one year! If I really have to answer this question, maybe I would like to see myself owning my own company and be my own boss in five years."

「五年後？我連自己一年後會變怎樣都不清楚！如果一定要回答這個問題，可能我想要看見自己五年後擁有自己的公司，當自己的老闆。」

② Show yourself in negative light.
給人不佳的形象。

例 "At this stage of my life, I have to struggle to make both ends meet and cannot plan for five years later."

「現階段我必須非常努力才能勉強收支平衡，無法計劃到五年後。」

③ **Seems lacking in ambition.**
顯得似乎缺乏企圖心。

 "Usually I do not plan my life that far ahead because it seldom turns out the way I want it to be. I can only take each day as it comes along."

「通常我不會計劃到那麼遠，因為我的生命很少能夠讓我做什麼規劃，我只能一天過一天。」

建議

① **Conservative yet positive answers.**
保守但正面的答案。

 "In the field of technology, everything develops very rapidly. I'd like to go back to the university on weekends to gain further knowledge. If I get the master degree in three years, I'll think about what to do."

「在科技這個領域，所有事物發展都非常快，我想利用周末回大學進修，三年後如果我得到碩士學位後，再來想想該做什麼。」

② **Ambitious answers.** 有抱負的答案。

 "It has been a long time since I have worked as a certified nurse in hospitals and clinics. In five year,

I want to run my own senior citizens' nursing home. If I am offered the job in your day care center of the elderly, I'll put all my efforts to work and learn for sure. You won't be disappointed."

「我在醫院與診所當合格護士已有很長一段時間，五年後我想要經營屬於我自己的銀髮族安養院。如果能有機會在你們銀髮族日間看護中心工作，我一定盡全力工作、學習，我不會讓你們感到失望的。」

③ Positive statements for the company.
對公司而言為正面的說法。

例 "I believe that I can learn and grow very fast in your company because it is the leading firm in this industry. In five years, I would like to see myself working in a managerial position in your company, leading highly capable teams. The contribution I would be making as an executive here would be far more than you can expect now."

「我相信我可以在貴公司中快速學習、成長，因為貴公司為業界龍頭，五年後我想要看見自己在你們公司的經理階層工作，帶領高能力的團隊，如果能於此擔任主管職位，我所能貢獻的遠比你們現在能期待的高得多。」

Unit
15 How much money do you want?

你的期望待遇是多少？

① Ask too much.
要求太高。

例 "I was paid 32000 Taiwan Dollars per month in the last Taiwanese company I worked for. Since this is an American company, I'd like to increase my monthly salary by 50%."

「我在上家台灣公司的月薪是 32000 元台幣，既然貴公司是家美商，我想要增加月薪 50%。」

② Do not do the homework.
不先做功課。

例 "Judging from my education background and work experiences, I think the starting pay as the sales assistant in this company should be at least 80000 Taiwan Dollars per month for me."

「從我的教育背景與工作經驗看來，我想我在這家公司當業務助理的起薪應該至少一個月要有八萬元台幣。」

③Demand unreasonable benefits.
要求的福利不合理。

（例） "Aside from my starting pay of 50000 Taiwan Dollars per month, every year I would like to have one-month paid holidays during the Lunar New Year."

「除了每月五萬元台幣的起薪，每年我都想要有農曆新年期間的一個月帶薪休假。」

建議

①Be somewhat reasonable and do some research.
合理一些，做點功課。

（例） "My last salary was 32000 Taiwan Dollars per month. According to friends of mine in this industry, this position now should be about 33000 to 36000 Taiwan Dollars."

「我上份工作月薪 32000 元台幣，根據我在業界工作的朋友，現在這樣的職位應該有 33000 到 36000 元台幣月薪。」

②Offer a range, not a specific number.
提供一個範圍，而不是一個確切數字。

（例） "I am not sure how much pay is acceptable but since my last salary was 32000 Taiwan Dollars per month, any pay above that would be fine to me."

「我不太清楚合宜的待遇該是多少，不過既然我上份工所的薪水是 32000 元台幣，只要能夠比 32000 元高我都能接受。」

③Pay attention to the benefits and the whole package.
注意福利與整體條件。

例 "Can the employees here get make-up holidays and year-end bonuses?"

「這裡的員工可以獲得補假與年終獎金嗎？」

三、情境對話 Situational Conversations

Ⓐ "Tell me about yourself in English."

Ⓑ "Sure. I was born in Taichung and finished my schooling there. Four years ago I came to Taipei to study International Trade at the university. Right after my graduation I did an internship in a trading company in the past six months. Now I am pretty familiar with the general business in an import & export company and would like to apply for the position of the sales assistant in your company."

Ⓐ "It seems this would be your first formal job you have applied for. Have you worked as a sales assistant before?"

Ⓑ "During my internship, I learned almost everything in the office."

Ⓐ "Since we have to train you in the beginning, are you all right with the pay of 28000 Dollars?"

Ⓑ "No problem. As time goes by, you'll notice how fast I learn things."

Ⓐ "In that case, I'll ask your supervisor to give you a raise accordingly. When can you start?"

Ⓑ "I can start at any time that suits you."

Ⓐ "See you next Monday then."

Ⓐ 「請用英語自我介紹一下。」

Ⓑ 「我出生於台中，在那兒完成了中小學教育，四年前我來到台北上大學，主修國際貿易，畢業之後，也就是在過去六個月，我在一家貿易公司當實習生，現在我對於進出口業務相當熟悉，想要申請貴公司的業務助理一職。」

Ⓐ 「這份工作似乎是您申請過的第一份正式工作，之前您當過業務助理嗎？」

B「在我實習期間，幾乎所有辦公室內的事我都學會了。」

A「因為一開始我們還要提供您教育訓練，28000元的待遇您可以接受嗎？」

B「沒問題，時間久了，您會注意到我學習得有多快。」

A「那樣的話，我會請您的主管視情況為您加薪。您何時可以開始上班？」

B「任何適合您的時間都可以。」

A「那麼下星期一見。」

四、字彙庫 Word Bank

internship [`ɪntɝnˌʃɪp] *n.*　　實習

position [pə`zɪʃən] *n.*　　職位，職務

assistant [ə`sɪstənt] *n.*　　助理

formal [`fɔrml̩] *a.*　　正式的

supervisor [ˌsupɚ`vaɪzɚ] *n.*　主管

raise [rez] *n.*　　加薪

accordingly [ə`kɔrdɪŋlɪ] *adv.* 照著；相應地

suit [sut] *v.*　　適合

貼 心 小 叮 嚀

Body Language 肢體語言

　　肢體語言非常重要，當肢體語言與口中所說出的詞語不符合時，一般的聽者會採信肢體語言，尤其是眼神所透露的訊息，因此在面試時一定要特別注意這一點。

The Tone 語調

　　把握「不卑不亢，溫柔而堅定」的原則，自然而然就能運用合宜的語調來表達內心真誠的感覺，而誠懇的態度是最能打動對方的方法。

Chapter 2

New Employee Orientation

新進員工訓練

一、簡介 Short Introduction

 16

　　好不容易通過了面試，順利進入了一家新公司，接著馬上要面臨的是新進員工訓練，許多企業還有試用期，新進員工在這段期間內，不但要克服不安全感，還要努力快速學習，以求得最佳表現。在一個說英語的辦公室環境中，除了自身英語問題外，還可能會有不少的文化差異問題，許許多多事情似乎毫無脈絡可循，什麼是該說的，什麼是不該說的，用英語又要如何表達才能顯得既不失禮又能精準到位，請看本章為這一個階段所整理的實用內容。

二、常用表達方式 Useful Expressions

你可能會聽到……

例 Everyone, this is our new【job title】.
　　各位，這位是我們的新【職銜】。

例 【Name】 is new to the company.
　　【姓名】是公司新進人員。

例 【Name】 is our new【job title】.
　　【姓名】是我們的新【職銜】。

例 This is【name】's first day working here.
　　今天是【姓名】在這裡工作的第一天。

例 Let's welcome 【name】 to join us.

讓我們歡迎【姓名】加入我們。

例 Welcome aboard..

歡迎加入。

例 It's good to have you with us.

很高興你能加入我們。

例 We look forward to working with you.

我們很期待能夠與你共事。

例 If you have any questions, just ask me.

如果你有任何問題，就儘管問我。

例 Please let me know if you need any help.

如果你需要任何協助，請讓我知道。

這時該問什麼？

MP3 17

Policies

政策

1. Working hours
工作時數

例 Do I have to punch in and out every day?
我需要每天打卡嗎？

例 Do I have to work overtime? How often?
我需要加班嗎？多常加班？

例 Is this job duty of responsibility?
這份工作是責任制嗎？

例 When is the lunch break?
幾點午休？

例 Will I get messages in LINE after working hours?
下班後我會收到 LINE 的訊息嗎？

2. Dress codes
服裝標準

例 What are dress codes like in this company?
公司有規定的服裝標準嗎？

例 Do I have to wear company uniforms?
我需要穿公司制服嗎？

例 Am I supposed to wear suits and ties?
我需要穿西裝打領帶嗎？

例 Shall I wear a white shirt with a tie?
我需要穿白襯衫打領帶嗎？

3. Computer & smart phone
電腦與智慧型手機

例 May I have a computer with a big screen to protect my eyesight?
我的電腦可以有大螢幕好保護我的視力嗎？

例 Could I use a smart phone at work?
我可以在工作時使用智慧型手機嗎？

例 Can we go out of the office to make a personal call?
我們可以到辦公室外講私人電話嗎？

例 Are we allowed to use the Internet during work?
我們可以在工作時上網嗎？

例 Do I have to join the group of the department in LINE?
我得要加入部門 LINE 的群組嗎？

Unit 2 Benefits
🎧 18

福利

---

1. Pay
薪水

例 Do I get paid for my overwork?
加班有加班費嗎？

例 How and when do I get my salary?
我的薪水是怎麼給付的，何時發薪水呢？

例 How can I get a raise?
我要如何才能獲得加薪？

例 Will I get extra money for support if I attend trade fairs abroad?
如果我到國外參展可以得到額外津貼嗎？

---

2. Benefits
福利

例 Do we have health insurance and labor insurance?
我們有健保和勞保嗎？

例 Do I have to apply for labor insurance myself?
我必須要自己申請勞保嗎？

例 Do you provide training courses or workshops?
你們是否會提供培訓課程或工作坊？

例 Do the staff here get discounts in the cafeteria?
這裡的員工在餐廳用餐是否享有折扣？

例 Do you arrange tours for the employees?
你們是否有安排員工旅遊？

3. Holidays
休假

例 Do you offer deferred holidays?
你們是否提供補假？

例 Can I decide when to take make-up holidays myself?
我是否可以自己決定何時補假？

例 What are the leave of absence procedures like?
請假的程序是怎麼樣的？

例 Do you provide maternal leaves? How long?
你們是否提供產假？多久呢？

例 Do male employees get paternal leaves here? How long?
男性員工是否有育嬰假？多久呢？

Unit 3 Performance Appraisal
表現評量

例 How am I going to be evaluated for my work?
我的工作會受到什麼樣的評量？

例 What is your performance appraisal like?
你們如何評量工作表現？

例 Will all my coworkers know my performance evaluation?
我所有的同事都會知道我的表現評量嗎？

例 Do I get a raise for my excellent performance?
我會因為表現傑出而得到加薪嗎？

例 Who will be evaluating my internship in the end?
誰會在我實習期結束後評量我的表現？

三、情境對話 Situational Conversations

A "Hi, I'm Monica from the Human Resources, and I'm here to give you a new employee orientation."

B "Hi, I'm Jack. It's nice to meet you."

A "Nice to meet you, too. Let me give you a tour of our office building."

B "That's very nice of you. Thank you."

A "This is the reception area for all visitors. This elevator will take us to the office."

B "It looks really bright here. This is such a huge and modern office."

A "Your workspace is over there."

B "I thought I would be working in a traditional cubical."

A "We prefer this sort of open office to encourage employees to engage with each other. It's much better to communicate face to face than sending e-mails."

B "I see your point."

A "Follow me this way. On your right hand side you can see the cafeteria and break areas."

B "I love this spacious dining hall with this cozy café. Look,the break areas are decorated with all sorts of green plants."

A "Our CEO thinks that it's important for all staff from different departments to mingle."

B "Wouldn't that take too much time out of their work?"

A "We think that in the advertisement business, it's important to be innovative. When people interact with each other, they are more likely to bring about creative ideas."

B "I couldn't agree more. This working environment here is really amazing."

A 「嗨,我是人力資源部門的莫妮卡,我來這裡是為了要為你提供新進員工訓練。」

B 「嗨,我叫傑克,很高興認識你。」

A 「嗨,我也很高興認識你,讓我帶你看看我們的辦公室大樓。」

B 「你真好,謝謝。」

A 「這裡是接待所有訪客的地方,這是到我們辦公室的電梯。」

B 「這裡看起來很明亮,這辦公室真是寬敞且現代。」

A 「你的工作區域就在那兒。」

B 「我以為我會在傳統辦公隔間工作。」

A 「我們比較喜歡這樣的開放式辦公室,以鼓勵員工彼此間的互動。面對面的溝通比寄電子郵件好很多。」

B 「我明白你的意思。」

A 「請跟我來,你可以在右手邊看到餐廳與休閒區。」

B「我很喜歡這個寬敞的用餐區和這溫馨的咖啡廳，你看，休閒區有好多綠色盆栽作裝飾。」

A「我們執行長認為各部門員工間的交流是很重要的。」

B「那樣不會花掉太多工作時間嗎？」

A「我們認為創新在廣告業很重要，人們有互動就較易產生具有創意的點子。」

B「我真的很同意這一點，這裡的工作環境真是太好了。」

四、字彙庫 Word Bank

orientation [ˌorɪɛnˋteʃən] *n.*	職前訓練	
reception [rɪˋsɛpʃən] *n.*	接待	
cubical [ˋkjubək!] *n.*	辦公隔間	
engage [ɪnˋgedʒ] *v.*	從事，參加	
cafeteria [ˌkæfəˋtɪrɪə] *n.*	自助食堂	
spacious [ˋspeʃəs] *a.*	寬敞的	
cozy [ˋkozɪ] *a.*	舒適的	
mingle [ˋmɪŋg!] *v.*	相混合；交往，往來	
innovative [ˋɪnoˌvetɪv] *a.*	創新的	

Show your passion 展現熱誠

　　在剛進公司時，最重要的是要展現對這份工作的熱誠，讓主管感受到你的強烈企圖心，同時表現你對公司的高度參與意願，還有可以與人合作良好的團隊精神。

Do not overemphasize benefits
不要過於強調福利

　　除了確定公司有提供基本的勞健保、喪假、產假、育嬰假等，不宜一開始就要求過高的福利，例如員工出國旅遊，這樣會給人留下太過在意報酬且不切實際的印象。

Avoid some sensitive questions
要避免一些敏感問題

　　剛開始於一家公司展開新工作，對許多全新的人事物可能都會產生好奇心，儘管如此，還是要盡量避免提出一些敏感問題，例如詢問周圍同事或主管的薪水多少，刺探他人的婚姻狀態，或者是否有男女朋友等交友情形，這些都是屬於私領域範圍，應該謹慎避開，以免一開始就給人留下不良印象，等到將來再想要扭轉某些負面印象可能不是那麼容易。

Chapter

3

Telephoning

電話用語

一、簡介 Short Introduction

　　剛開始學習用英語講電話時，有一些固定的用法需要學習，通常只要稍加練習，馬上就可以上手，多次演練後，就完全習慣成自然。英語商務電話用語比一般的電話通話內容更強調精簡，除了掌握基本英語電話慣用語，於電話中用英語洽談商業事項時，還有不少細節需要特別注意，本章將英語電話步驟一一分解，並且詳盡解說，讀者只要詳加閱讀，多方應用，不斷修正自己從前常會犯的錯誤，就不會有一遇到要用英語講電話就手忙腳亂的情形發生了。

二、常用表達方式 Useful Expressions　🎧 20

這時該怎麼說？

Unit
1 Starting the conversation

開始對話

---

1. Taking a call
接電話

> (Company name) (your name) speaking, how can I help you?
> 這裡是【公司名稱】的【你的名字】，有什麼需要我服務的？

例 Philips, James Chang speaking, how can I help you?
這裡是菲利浦的張健士，有什麼需要我服務的？

> Good morning, (Company name) (your name) speaking.
> 早安，這裡是【公司名稱】的【你的名字】。

例 Good morning, Philips, James Chang speaking.
早安，這裡是菲利浦的張健士。

2. Making a call
打電話

Hello, this is (your name) from (company).
哈囉，我是【公司名稱】的【你的名字】。

例 Hello, this is James Chang from Philips.
哈囉，我是菲利浦的張健士。

Hello, this is (your name) speaking.
哈囉，我是【你的名字】。

例 Hello, this is James speaking.
哈囉，我是健士。

3. Asking for somebody
找他人

例 May I speak to Mr. Lee, please?
請問我可以和李先生通電話嗎？

例 Could I speak to Mr. Lee, please?
請問我可以和李先生通電話嗎？

例 I'd like to speak to Mr. Lee, please.
我想和李先生通電話。

4. Answering the phone and confirming that you are speaking
接電話並確認你是對方要找的人

Speaking.　　　　　　　　我就是。

Ⓐ Hello, may I speak to Mr. Huang?
「哈囉，請問我可以和黃先生通電話嗎？」

Ⓑ Yes, speaking.
「我就是。」

---

5. Reasons for calling.
打電話的理由

例 I was wondering if you could tell me...
不知道是否可以請您告訴我……

例 Could you tell me...
不知道能不能告訴我……

例 I'm calling to...
我打電話來是想……

Unit

2 Asking to be called back, leaving or taking a message

🎵 MP3 21

請對方回電話、留話或傳話

---

1. Taking a message
留話

例 Mr. Huang is not available at the moment.
- Can I take a message for you?
- Would you like me to take a message?
- Would you like to leave a message?

黃先生現在不方便聽電話，
--我可以幫您留話嗎？
--您想要我幫您留話嗎？
--您想要留話嗎？

---

2. Asking to leave a message
要求留話

例 I'd like to leave him/her a message.
我想要留話給他／她。

例 Would you mind taking a message?
你可否幫我留話？

例 Could you please taking a message for me?

可否請你幫我留話？

3. Passing on the message
   傳話

例 I'll let him/her know you called.
我會告訴他／她您打來過。

例 I'll ask him/her to call you back.
我會請他／她回您電話。

例 I'll make sure he/she gets your message.
我一定會讓他／她收到您的留言。

例 I'll pass the message on to him/her.
我會將留言傳給他／她。

4. Asking to the caller to call back
   請打電話來者再打一次

例 He is in a meeting now.
-Would you mind calling back later?
-Please call back after 11 o'clock.

他現在正在開會，
--您要不要晚點再打來？
--請於十一點後再打來。

3 Connecting and asking to be connected

MP3 22

接通，要求接通

1. Asking someone to hold
要求某人等待

例 One moment please.
請等一下。

例 Wait a moment please.
請等一下。

例 I'll just put you on hold for a moment.
請您等一下。

例 May I put you on hold for a moment?
我可以請您等一下嗎？

2. Asking to be connected
要求接通

例 Could you connect me to the director's office, please?"
請幫我轉接主任辦公室。

例 Could you please put me through to Mary Wang, the Sales Department?
請幫我轉接業務部王瑪莉。

例 Can you transfer me to Mr. Richardson?
請幫我轉接李查森先生好嗎？

3. Connecting someone
　　接通某人

例 Just a moment please, I'll connect you.
請等一下，我為您轉接。

例 One moment please, I'll put you through.
請等一下，我為您轉接。

例 She is not here now. Please dial the extension number 12.
她現在不在這裡，請撥分機號碼12。
Please dial 9 and someone will assist you.
請撥9，有專人會為您服務。

例 I'm his assistant. He is not available at the moment. If there is anything urgent, you can let me know.
我是他的助理，他現在不在這裡，如果有任何急事可以告訴我。

例 She is on vacation. Would you like to leave a message?
她在度假中，您想要留個訊息嗎？

Unit 4 Ending the call

🎧 23

結束通話

例 Give my regards to...
請代我向某人問候。

例 Thank you very much for your help.
感謝您給我的幫忙。

例 Thank you (Thanks) for calling.
謝謝來電。

例 Thank you for your time.
謝謝您的寶貴時間。

例 Speak to you soon.
希望很快再聯絡。

例 Take care, bye.
保重，再見。

三、情境對話 Situational Conversations

Mr. Liu: "This is Deming Liu from Shiny Star Agency in Hong Kong. Could you please put me through to Ms. Wang, the Sales Department?"

Operator: Sure. Just a moment please."

Ms. Wang: "This is Mary Wang speaking. How can I help you?"

Mr. Liu: I am David Li's agent, Deming Liu. On the 3th of July Mr. Li is supposed to fly from Hong Kong to Taipei for a CD signing event on the 4th of July, but today I found on your website the date of the event was the 6th of July. This is a huge mistake because on the 6th of July Mr. Li is scheduled to fly from Taipei to Seoul in the early morning."

Ms. Wang: "Really? What could we do now? Is it possible for you to change the date? We have organized everything months ago."

Mr. Liu: "Could you connect me to the director's office, please?"

Ms. Wang: "Yes. One moment please."

Mr. Liu: "Mr. Ma, could you please fix the problem of the date? On the contract it is black-and-white there: the 4th of July. There is only one week before the event. This mistake is very serious."

Director: "Sorry to hear about that. Mary Wang is the new event coordinator in this company, and we're really sorry for this mistake she made. The CD signing event will take place on the 4th of July as we agreed, of course. I'll take care of everything. After the event, please let me treat you and Mr. David Li in a world-class restaurant in the Taipei 101 to make up for this."

Mr. Liu: "Thank you very much for your help."

劉先生：「我是香港閃星經紀公司的劉德明，請幫我接業務部門的王小姐。」

接線生：「沒問題，請等一下。」

王小姐：「我是王瑪莉，請問有什麼需要我服務的呢？」

劉先生：「我是李大衛的經紀人劉德明，在七月三日李先生預計要從香港飛往台北，參加七月四日的CD簽名會，但是今天我在你們網站發現活動的日期是七月六日，這個錯誤很嚴重，因為李先生預計於七月六日清晨從台北飛往首爾。」

王小姐：「真的嗎？那我們現在能做什麼？你們可以改日期嗎？我們好幾個月前就安排好了所有事項。」

劉先生：「請幫我轉接主任辦公室。」

王小姐：「好，請等一下。」

劉先生：「馬先生，請處理一下日期的問題好嗎？在合約上白紙黑字寫著：七月四日，距離活動只有一個星期，這個錯誤很嚴重。」

主任：「真遺憾聽到這樣的事，王瑪莉是這家公司新來的活動聯絡人，我們對於她所犯的錯誤感到很抱歉，我們當然會如同我們所約定的，於七月四日舉行CD簽名會，我會處理所有的事項，活動後請讓我請您與李大衛到台北101的世界級餐廳用餐以彌補這個錯誤。」

<u>劉先生</u>：「多謝您的幫忙。」

四、字彙庫 Word Bank

agency [`edʒənsɪ] *n.*　　　　經紀公司

agent [`edʒənt] *n.*　　　　經紀人

suppose [sə`poz] *v.*　　　　假定

schedule [`skɛdʒʊl] *v.*　　　　安排

coordinator [ko`ɔrdn͵etɚ] *n.*　協調者

contract [kən`trækt] *n.*　　　合約

world-class [`wɝld͵klæs] *a.*　世界級的

Write down your main points first 先寫下重點

　　在打電話前先寫下重點有助於組織思想，與對方對答時思路才能保持清晰，這樣也就不會浪費彼此的時間了。

Speak slowly 慢慢說

　　從容不迫慢慢地將自己的話有條理地說出，可以讓電話那一端的聽者較不受到自己的腔調干擾，同時也較不需要重覆，避免對方產生誤解；特別需要放慢速度說的是關於時間與金錢的數字，如果對方講得太快，也可以請對方將數字重覆一遍。

Ask to slow down and repeat 要求說慢一點，再說一次

　　如果實在不能了解對方的意思，可以要求對方放慢速度，再重覆一遍，大多數人都能體諒這一點，樂於幫助你理解對話內容。

Chapter 4

Presentation

簡報

一、簡介 Short Introduction

做商務簡報是一門大學問，更何況是用英語來做簡報。因為篇幅有限，本章的設計是以一問一答的方式來介紹做英語簡報的幾個大原則，希望這樣提綱挈領的方式能夠回答讀者可能有的問題，也能夠重點式提供英語簡報的技巧。每個人喜歡的簡報方式雖然可能都不盡相同，各人的英語表達風格也因人而異，如能靈活運用本章中的內容必可為你的簡報增添色彩。

二、常用表達方式 Useful Expressions

 24

關於如何做簡報的問&答

Unit

1 Content of the presentation

簡報內容

1.

How should I start my presentation?
我該如何展開一場簡報?

Answer

☞ You can begin the presentation with a good question, a meaningful story or a famous statement.
你可以用一個好問題、一個有意義的故事,或是引用名言來展開一場簡報。

例 You can say: "Let me tell you what happened to me."
你可以說:「讓我告訴你們一件發生在我身上的事。」

2.

How should I prepare the PowerPoint?
我該如何準備投影片?

Answer

☞ Do not put too many words on one slide of PowerPoint.
一張投影片上不要放太多的字。

☞ It's a good idea to use bullet points to state the main points.
可以在每個要點前使用重點記號標示。

例 You can say: "Please look at the main points of my presentation."
你可以說：「請看一下我簡報的重點。」

Question 3.

Should I make a small card of main points to remind myself?
我該做張寫有重點的小卡來提醒自己嗎？

Answer

☞ Avoid taking a small piece of paper on the stage to be natural.
避免在台上拿張小紙條，這樣看起來比較自然。

例 You can say: "A picture speaks a thousand words. Please take a look at some of the great photos I shot during my research in China."

你可以說：「百聞不如一見，請大家看看我在中國研究時所拍的一些精彩照片。」

4.

How should I end the presentation?"
我該如何結束簡報？

Answer

☞ It is advisable that you end the presentation with a general conclusion or a serious statement.
建議用總結或嚴肅的言論來結束簡報。

例 You can say: "In the end, I would like to remind you: Change or you will be changed."
你可以說：「最後，我想要提醒大家：現在就做改變，不然將來你會被迫做改變。」

Unit 2 Your body language

🔊 25

你的肢體語言

1.

Where should I stand?

我該站在哪兒？

Answer

☞ There are no specific rules of where you should stand.

關於你該站在什麼地方，沒有什麼特別的規定。

☞ It is a good idea to get rid of a podium.

可以將講台拿開。

例 You can say: "I hope you don't mind that I walk around while talking to you."

你可以說：「我希望你們不介意我一邊走一邊與你們說話。」

2.

How should I use my eye contact?

我該如何運用我的眼神接觸？

Answer

☞ Be natural and glance at all the listeners.
自然地掃視所有聽眾。

☞ Never stare at the back wall during the presentation.
千萬不要在簡報中一直盯著後面的牆壁看。

例 You can say: "I hope all of you can see me clearly."
你可以說：「我希望你們都可以清楚看到我。」

Question 3.

How should I use my hand gestures?
我該如何使用手勢？

Answer

☞ Do not put your hand in the pocket of your pants.
不要將你的手放在褲子口袋中。

☞ Use natural gestures and avoid pointing at the audience.
使用自然的手勢，避免用手指著觀眾。

例 You can say: "Maybe I should avoid pointing at anyone here in case someone thinks I am referring to him."
你可以說：「或許我應該要避免手指著這裡的任何人，以免有人以為我的話是針對他所說的。」

Unit 3 Getting the audience involved

MP3 26

讓聽眾參與

1.

How to get the audience involved?
我該如何讓聽眾參與呢？

Answer

☞ You can tell a joke or a story, ask questions, show a short film related to your topic.
你可以說個笑話或故事，問問題，放段與你主題有關的短片。

例 You can say: "I'd like to share a joke with you, and remember there is some truth in all jokes."
你可以說：「我想要與你們分享一個笑話，要記住所有的笑話都帶點真實性。」

2.

How to get the audience to answer my questions?"
我該如何讓聽眾回答我的問題呢？

Answer

☞ You can raise interesting questions and prepare small gifts for the listeners who answer your questions.
你可以提出有意思的問題，為回答你的問題的聽眾準備小禮物。

例 You can say: "Whoever has the correct answer to this question will get this small gift."

你可以說：「誰答對了這問題就可以得到這一個小禮物。」

三、情境對話 Situational Conversations

Host: "On behalf of the department of English Studies, I'd like to welcome Mr. Lin to give us a presentation."

Guest speaker: "Today I would like to talk about the safety of taking working holidays abroad. Each year hundreds and thousands of young people applying for working holidays overseas. Many of them have vague ideas of their target countries in mind before their departure. Some might learn the language of the country, such as English and Japanese; some might take a crash course of the culture of their destination. Take the example of Australia, many young workers on working holidays from Taiwan do not realize the hardship on the farms before they're sent to work there. Please take a look at some of the photos of workers taken on the farm in Queensland. Very often they are not properly insured, and the local labor law might not be able to protect them. When there are disputes with the employers,they often have nobody to seek help from. I would like to advise those young people who are interested in going on working holidays abroad to gather as much information as possible. It's very helpful to ask advice from the people who recently returned from that place. Doing adequate homework before you leave can reduce many problems for you and your family."

<u>主持人</u>：「在此我代表英文系歡迎林先生來為我們做一場簡報。」

<u>特邀演講者</u>：「今天我想要來談談海外打工度假的安全。每年都有無數的年輕人申請海外打工度假，其中很多人在出國前對他們要去的國家了解非常有限，有些人可能會學習當地的語言，例如英語和日語；有些人可能會上個關於目的地文化的速成班。就拿澳洲來說，很多來自台灣的打工度假年輕人在被送到那兒前對農場的艱辛毫無概念。請看看這幾張在昆士蘭農場上的工人照片，這些人很多沒有足夠的保險，當地的勞工法律可能無法保護他們；當與雇主發生糾紛時，他們往往求助無門。我希望想要申請海外打工度假的年輕人盡可能收集足夠資訊，多方諮詢剛從當地回來的人非常有用，在出發前做足功課可以為你與你的家人減少很多問題。」

四、字彙庫 Word Bank

behalf [bɪˋhæf] *n.*　　　　代表；利益（用於慣用語）

vague [veg] *a.*　　　　模糊不清的

target [ˋtɑrgɪt] *n.*　　　　（欲達到的）目標

destination [ˌdɛstəˋneʃən] *n.*　目的地

hardship [ˋhɑrdʃɪp] *n.*　　艱難，困苦

insure [ɪnˋʃʊr] *v.*　　　　為……投保

gather [ˋgæðɚ] *v.*　　　　收集

adequate [ˋædəkwɪt] *a.*　　足夠的

reduce [rɪˋdjus] *v.* 減　　少；降低

貼心小叮嚀

Body Language 肢體語言

　　簡報時的肢體語言極為重要，無論是選擇在講台上來回踱步，或是運用手勢，加上面部表情，目的都是為了要能讓觀眾為這場簡報加分，而想要讓聽眾感到自在，首先要讓自己完全融入這場簡報。

The control of timing 時間控制

　　時間控制合宜能讓聽眾對於這場簡報起共鳴，結束後聽眾也會對充實的內容回味無窮；相反的，如果時間控制不佳，聽者則會感到疲憊或乏味。如果能將時間拿捏得恰到好處，也就將聽眾反應掌握大半了。

Chapter

5

On a Business Trip

出差

一、簡介 Short Introduction

　　到英語系國家出差聽起來是件令人感到愉快的事，但是要如何在整個過程中，用英語打點好出國所有大小事，並且順利完成公司交辦事項，令所接觸過的對象都對你留下良好的深刻印象，這可就需要具備一定的英語程度，才能充分發揮應變能力來完成使命；即使如此，也不要因此就對需要用到英語的出差任務打退堂鼓，因為只要將本章內容好好學起來，英語就不再是到外國商務旅行的絆腳石，反而立刻化身為墊腳石。

二、常用表達方式 Useful Expressions

 27

這時該怎麼說？

Unit

1 **Passing the Customs**

過海關

示範對話：

Question 1.

Do you have anything to declare?
您有東西要申報嗎？

Answer

☞ I have nothing to declare.
我沒有東西要申報。

Question 2.

What is the purpose of your visit?
您來這裡目的為何？

Answer

☞ I'm here on business.
我是來出差。

Where do you plan to stay? And for how long?
您計畫待在哪裡？待多久？

Answer

☞ I'll stay at the Sheraton Hotel in downtown Boston for two weeks.
我會在波士頓市中心的喜來登飯店住兩星期。

Unit

2 At the Bank

🎧 28

在銀行

示範對話：

A I'd like to change some money.
我想要換點錢。

B How would you like to have your money changed?
您想要怎麼樣換錢？

A I'd like to change this into the U.S. dollar, please.
請將這些錢換成美元。

B No problem.
沒問題。

A What's the exchange rate for the U.S. dollar?
現在美元的匯率如何？

3 Taking a Taxi

🎵 **MP3** 29

搭計程車

示範對話：

🅐 Please take me to the Sheraton Hotel in downtown Boston.

請載我到波士頓市中心的喜來登飯店。

🅑 There are two Sheraton Hotels in downtown Boston. Which one are you going to?

波士頓市中心共有兩家喜來登飯店，您要到哪一家去？

🅐 Let me show you the map on my smart phone. This is the one, please.

請看我智慧型手機上的地圖，這家就是我要去的。

🅑 No problem.

沒問題。

🅐 May I have a receipt afterwards?

等一下我可以要一張收據嗎？

🅑 Of course.

當然可以。

Unit 4 In a Hotel

🎵 30

在飯店

示範對話：

Question 1.

How can I help you?
有什麼需要我服務的？

Answer

☞ I'd like to check in, please. This is my passport, and I have a reservation for 5 nights.
我想要登記入住，這是我的護照，我預約了五晚的房間。

Question 2.

I'd like to treat a client in the restaurant in this hotel. Which one would you recommend?
我想要請我的客戶在這家飯店內的餐廳吃飯，您會推薦哪一家呢？

Answer

☞ Our Italian restaurant on the third floor is quite famous.
我們三樓的義大利餐廳十分有名。

Unit
5 **Meeting a Client**
與客戶會面

示範對話：

1. Opening the conversation (Small talk)
開始對話（閒聊）

例 Hi, we haven't seen each other for a long time. How are you doing?
嗨，我們很久沒見面了，您好嗎？

例 How are things?
一切還好嗎？

例 How have you been?
您最近好嗎？

例 How are you getting on with that issue?
那件事情處理得怎麼樣了？

2. Main discussion
主要談話內容

例 How is the business?
工作還好嗎？

例 Let's go straight to business.
讓我們直接開始談正事。

例 Let's get down to business.
讓我們開始談正事。

例 What brought you here?
您來這裡的目的為何？

例 Do you mind if I start to talk about it?
您介意我開始談這件事嗎？

3. Ending the conversation
結束對話

例 Thank you for this fruitful meeting
這場會談非常有成果，謝謝您。

例 Thank you for your time.
謝謝您寶貴的時間。

例 I'm glad we agree on so many points.
我很高興我們對很多事項有相同的觀點。

例 It's been great talking to you face to face.
很高興能與您面對面討論事情。

6 Company Visit MP3 32

拜訪公司

示範對話：

1. Touring the company
參觀公司

例 Could you please give us a tour of your office building?
可以麻煩帶我們參觀一下您的辦公室大樓嗎？

例 What is the purpose of this huge hall?
這間大廳是用來做什麼的呢？

例 Where is the meeting room?
會議室在哪邊？

例 What a fantastic multi-functional space!
真是個美好的多功能空間！

2. Meeting the people
與人會面

例 You must be the Director, Mr. Anderson.
您一定就是主任安德森先生。

例 It's my pleasure to meet you, Mr. Anderson.
安德森先生，認識您是我的榮幸。

例 Finally I can put a face to every name.
總算可以將面孔與每個名字連上了。

3. Ending the company visit
結束拜訪公司

例 Thank you for hosting me today.
謝謝您今天接待我。

例 It's my pleasure to pay a visit to your company.
來貴公司拜訪是我的榮幸。

例 All of you have done a good job to give me a tour of your company.
你們都很認真帶我參觀貴公司。

例 You are always welcome to visit our headquarter in Taiwan.
您隨時都可以來我們台北總公司參觀。

三、情境對話 Situational Conversations

A "How was your flight?"

B "The flight was delayed for about 3 hours, and the transfer in Hawaii was late as well; flight attendants were rude. Aside from that, it was all right."

A "How is the service of the hotel you're staying?"

B "The room is small and damp, and the fridge is broken. Other than that, it is a decent hotel."

A "How long are you going to stay in Boston this time?"

B "Five days. During this stay here I have to visit seven companies."

A "In that case, let's head towards the factory now to save time."

B "Please lead the way."

A "This factory has been running for more than thirty years."

B "It seems quite old."

A "We update our equipment constantly. Many helpful tools are imported from your country to improve efficiency on the production lines."

B "This time I brought our latest robots to demonstrate to you."

A "I can't wait to see!"

Ⓐ 「旅途好嗎？」

Ⓑ 「航班延誤了約三小時，在夏威夷的轉機也耽擱了，空中服務員很沒禮貌，除此以外，都還好。」

Ⓐ 「您待的旅館服務如何？」

Ⓑ 「房間很小而且潮濕，電冰箱壞了，除此之外，還算是家可以的旅館。」

Ⓐ 「這次您要在波士頓待多久？」

Ⓑ 「五天，在這裡的這段期間我必須拜訪七家公司。」

Ⓐ 「既然如此，讓我們現在往工廠的方向前進，才不會浪費時間。」

Ⓑ 「請帶路吧。」

Ⓐ 「這家工廠已經營運了超過三十年。」

Ⓑ 「看起來很老舊。」

Ⓐ 「我們經常更新我們的設備，很多實用的工具都是由貴國進口的，目的是要改善生產線的效率。」

Ⓑ 「這次我帶了我們最新的機器人來展示給您看。」

Ⓐ 「我等不及想看一看！」

四、字彙庫 Word Bank

transfer [træns`fɚ] *n.*	轉機
decent [`disnt] *a.*	還不錯的；像樣的、體面的
update [ʌp`det] *v.*	更新
constantly [`kɑnstənt] *adv.*	不斷地，持續地
efficiency [ɪ`fɪʃənsɪ] *n.*	效率；效能；功效
robot [`robət] *n.*	機器人
demonstrate *v.*	示範操作（產品），展示

貼 心 小 叮 嚀

Know your goals before the business trip
出差前確立目標

出發之前務必仔細思索此次出差所要達成的使命，通常不外乎是蒐集市場資訊、拓展國外市場、代表公司拜會國際合作夥伴，只要於出發前做足功課，例如好好準備所要討論的專案，那麼就不會有太大的問題了。

Keep fit during the business trip 出差期間保持體力

因為出差期間的作息與平時差異極大，所以要特別注意將體力調整好，帶好個人的藥品和維他命，多喝水，有機會多運動，掌握好在國外生活的節奏，適時休息，才能有最佳的表現。

Keep in touch after the business trip 出差後勤加聯絡

回國後儘快與在海外接觸過的客戶與廠商主動聯絡，謝謝對方的招待，這樣有助於加深對方對你的好印象，因為你所代表的是你的公司。除此之外，儘早主動對主管提出此行的成果報告，必定可以為自己大大加分。

Chapter

6

Touring a Trade Fair

參觀商展

一、簡介 Short Introduction

　　參觀商展看似容易，但是爲何每個人參觀之後的收獲往往有天壤之別？這當中與個人所做的功課有很大的關聯，特別是在參加官方語言爲英語的商展，更需要花些工夫去準備，首先必須要好好熟悉所要參展的廠商，確立此行想要達到的目標；接著，設想在這些情境下可能會要用到的英語表達方式，讀者可以就本章所提供的方向去做延伸，發展成適合特定產業的個人參展必備英文知識庫。請記住：機會總是留給準備得最好的人。

二、常用表達方式 Useful Expressions 33

這時該怎麼説？

Unit 1 In the beginning of the tour
參觀開始

1. **Is there anything special you are looking for?**
   您有特別在找什麼嗎？

2. **What in particular would you like to see this time?**
   這次您有什麼特別想看的嗎？

3. **Are you interested in something particular in this fair?**
   您對這次商展有什麼特別感興趣的嗎？

4. **Would you like to follow the floor plan to go through the fair?**
   您想遵循這張平面圖來參觀商展嗎？

Unit 2 In the middle of the tour

參觀當中

1. **How do you like this section of the exhibition?**
您喜歡展覽的這一區嗎？

2. **What is your opinion of this company?**
您對這家公司的看法如何？

3. **Would you like to move on to the next area?**
您想要走到下一區了嗎？

4. **Let's go to the next section over that corner.**
讓我們到轉角的下一區。

Unit 3 Introducing the guest to suitable Partners

MP3 35

將客人介紹給合適的夥伴

1. It's my pleasure to introduce you to Mr. Chen.

介紹您給陳先生認識是我的榮幸。

2. You wouldn't want to miss meeting Mr. Chen.

您絕對不想錯過認識陳先生的機會。

3. This is the Director of this trade fair, Mr. Chen.

這位是這場商展的主任陳先生。

4. You would definitely want to meet Mr. Chen.

您一定會想認識陳先生。

Unit

4 **In the end of the tour** MP3 36

參觀結束後

---

1. Did you enjoy this trade fair?
您是否喜歡這場商展？

---

2. What is your opinion on this exhibition?
您對這場商展的看法如何？

---

3. Would you like to visit the fair again next year?"
明年您還想再來參觀這商展嗎？

---

4. How does this computer exhibition compare with that in the States?
這場電腦展和美國的比起來如何？

三、情境對話 Situational Conversations

A "Are you interested in anything specifically in this book fair?"

B "Yes, I'm looking for books on interior design."

A "In that case, we should go straight to the end of section B. Please follow me."

B "Look. These books on café interior design look really professional."

A "Let me introduce you to the Rights Director of this publishing company, Ms. Wang."

B "Nice to meet you, Ms. Wang."

C "Nice to meet you, too."

B "This is my business card, please."

C "And this is mine. Thank you."

B "Your design books look so outstanding, especially those on café interior design."

C "Thank you. Are you an interior designer as well?"

B "Yes, I've done the designing for several shops."

A "At the moment, he also works as an art consultant for quite a few publishing companies in France."

B "I'd appreciate the opportunity to study Eastern interior design properly."

C "These two books on Japanese garden might be of interest to you."

B "Thank you. In the past few days, I've found some shops with small lovely gardens in Taipei."

C "It's a bit noisy here. Would you two like to talk with me over coffee outside of the exhibition hall?"

B "Of course, that's very nice of you. Thank you."

C "Thank you."

A 「這次書展你有什麼特別感興趣的嗎？」

B 「有的，我在找室內設計的書。」

A 「既然如此，我們應該直接到B區底去，請跟我來。」

B 「你看，這些關於咖啡屋室內設計的書看來真是專業。」

A 「讓我為你介紹這家出版社的版權主任王小姐。」

B 「很高興認識您，王小姐。」

C 「我也很高興認識您。」

B 「這是我的名片。」

C 「這是我的名片，謝謝。」

B 「你們的設計書看起來真的好傑出，特別是那些關於咖啡屋室內設計的書。」

C「謝謝，您也是室內設計師嗎？」

B「是的，我為幾家商店做過設計。」

A「現在他也擔任法國好幾家出版社的藝術顧問。」

B「我想把握機會好好研究東方的室內設計。」

C「這兩本日本庭園的書您或許會感興趣。」

B「謝謝。過去這幾天，我在台北發現了幾家有可愛小庭園的店家。」

C「這裡有點吵，你們兩位是否想與我到展場外一邊喝咖啡一邊談呢？」

B「當然好，謝謝您的好心，謝謝。」

C「謝謝。」

四、字彙庫 Word Bank

fair [fɛr] *n.*	商展	
interior [ɪn`tɪrɪɚ] *a.*	內部的	
professional [prə`fɛʃən!] *a.*	專業的	
outstanding [`aʊt`stændɪŋ] *a.*	傑出的	
consultant [kən`sʌltənt] *n.*	顧問	
exhibition [ɛksə`bɪʃn] *n.*	展覽；展覽會，展示會	
hall [hɔl] *n.*	會堂，大廳	

貼 心 小 叮 嚀

Do your research 做好功課

　　參觀商展前務必要做足功課，包含來訪客人的目標與參展廠商的資料，明瞭商展攤位平面圖的配置，展場周圍的公共設施，還有附近可帶客戶去進一步洽談的餐廳。如果能將一天的流程都事先安排好，那麼如果遇到突發狀況就更知道如何應變了。

Look for suitable partners carefully 嚴選合作對象

　　是否能夠將客戶與適合的公司或廠商做媒合，可說是決定了日後合作成敗的關鍵，因此事前必須要蒐集足夠的資訊，如此才更有機會創造雙贏局面，贏得更多商機。

Keep in touch afterwards 之後勤加聯絡

　　在展場上雖然與對方相談甚歡，彼此留下良好的印象，但是商展結束後如果不儘快聯絡，不久後就很有可能會忘記對方，因此不要嫌麻煩，主動寫封致謝的電子郵件，日後才能有更頻繁的互動，更有合作成功的機會。

Discrimination in the Workplace

職場上的歧視

一、簡介 Short Introduction

　　本章的議題是職場上的歧視，這個問題相當複雜，因此內容以個案研討的方式來呈現，希望藉由具體的例子可以刺激讀者去思考，在自己或親友的身上是否發生過類似的情形，在那些情況下要說些什麼才合宜，如果要用英語來準確表達個人的意見，又該如何說？本章的例子可以供作讀者參考，畢竟要能充分反映出自己的意見，又不會傷到他人的自尊，常常不是那麼容易，而且因職銜地位高低不同，每個人也會有不同的表達方式，讀者可以一邊讀本章一邊發展出自己的風格。

二、常用表達方式 Useful Expressions 37

這時該怎麼說？

Unit 1 Sex Discrimination

性別歧視

Case 1.

Your employer hasn't given you a promotion to the position of manager while two of your male colleagues in the same rank were recently promoted to managers. You suspect it has something to do with the fact you are female. What would you say?

你的雇主沒有將你升為經理，但是你的兩位男性同級同事最近卻升作經理，你懷疑這和你身為女性有關，你會怎麼說？

你可以這麼說

"Please take a close look at my work performance. Do you think that I am not good enough to be promoted to a manager or is it because this company is not ready for a female manager yet?"

「請仔細看看我的工作表現，您認為是我表現不夠好而不能被升為經理，還是這家公司還沒準備好有女性當經理？」

Unit 2 **Age Discrimination**

年齡歧視

38

Case 2.

Your interviewer does not employ you and say it is because you are a mature worker and you'll soon retire."

你的面試官沒有雇用你，說是因為你年紀太大，很快就會退休。

你 可 以 這 麼 說

"Based on my professional experiences, I am the best candidate for this position, and I can submit the result of my recent health check to prove my good health condition. Whether a person is young or old depends on his physical and mental states. As far as I am concerned, I have no plan to retire in the near future."

「從我的專業經歷看來，我是這職位的最佳人選，我可以提供最近的健康檢查結果來證明我的健康狀況良好。一個人算是年輕還是年老，要看他的生理和心理狀況而定，就我而言，我沒有要在近期內退休的打算。」

Case 3

The employer does not provide training opportunities for you and say it is not worth it because you'll quickly move on to another job. You assume it has much to do with your young age.

你的雇主不提供培訓計劃給你，說是因為你可能很快就會去找別的工作，所以不值得，你推定這很可能和你太年輕有關。

▶ 你可以這麼說

"I might not have many years of experiences in this field, but I am very motivated to learn. Please train me just like any others, and I'll soon prove to you it's all worthwhile."

「或許我在這個領域沒有很多年的經驗，但是我有非常強烈的學習動力，請一視同仁地訓練我，我很快就會證明給您看，這一切都是值得的。」

Unit
3 **Racial Discrimination**

 39

種族歧視

Case 4

You have worked in an American company as a country manager in Taiwan for four years, and it is very likely you'll be promoted to be the general manager for the whole Asian regions. Yet at the last minute the position is given to David, an American, who is obvious less qualified and experienced than you. You assume that decision is much related to your Taiwanese nationality. How would you approach this matter with your supervisor?

你在一家美國公司的擔任台灣總經理有四年之久,非常有可能會被升遷為全亞洲地區的總經理,但是在最後一刻,大衛得到這職位,他是一個美國人,比起你來說明顯較不勝任,資歷較淺,你推定這個決定與你的台灣國籍有很大的關係,你會如何和你的主管談這件事?

▶ 你可以這麼說

"Judging from the qualifications and experiences, all staff in this company would regard me as a much better candidate than David. May I ask if this decision might have something to do with our races? The manager of the whole Asian regions must have a deep understanding of all different Asian cultures, and that's exactly where my strength lies. Besides, I had altogether seven years of working experiences in quite a few multinational companies in the States. Please take all these facts into your reconsideration. Thank you."

「從資格和經驗看來，全公司的人都會認為我比大衛還更該得到這個職位，我想請問這個決定是否和我們的種族有關？全亞洲地區的經理必須對所有不同的亞洲文化有深度了解，這正是我的強項。除此以外，我曾在美國好幾家跨國公司工作過，總共長達七年之久，請將這些事實都都納入重新評估的考量範圍。謝謝。」

三、情境對話 Situational Conversations

Boss: "Can I add you in LINE? In our company we have group discussions in LINE quite often."

Eileen: "Sorry I don't have LINE."

Boss: "You can download it for free, you know."

Eileen: "At the moment I don't have a smart phone."

Boss: "How could that be? How can you survive without a smart phone these days?"

Eileen: "People who want to contact me usually just call me. Frankly speaking, I don't have so many friends who contact me constantly anyway. For me, privacy is much more important than anything else."

Boss: "Don't you check your FB sometimes?"

Eileen: "What is FB?"

Boss: "Facebook, of course. You do use Facebook, right?"

Eileen: "Oh, no. I don't think it is clever to put all your photos online for everyone to see and comment on."

Boss: "In that case, I think you might be too old to work here."

Eileen: "Wait a minute! Didn't you just say I could start working tomorrow?"

Boss: "Sorry about changing my mind, but I doubt you could fit in with other dynamic and young staff."

Eileen: "But…"

老闆：「我可以加你作LINE的好友嗎？我們公司很常在LINE進行群組討論。」

艾琳：「不好意思，我沒有LINE。」

老闆：「可以免費下載，這個你知道吧。」

艾琳：「目前我沒有智慧型手機。」

老闆：「怎麼可能？現在沒有智慧型手機怎麼有辦法生存？」

艾琳：「要聯絡我的人通常都會直接打電話給我，老實說，我也沒有那麼多會經常聯絡我的朋友。對我來說，隱私權是最重要的。」

老闆：「難道妳不會有時候要查一下FB？」

艾琳：「什麼是FB？」

老闆：「當然就是臉書。妳使用臉書吧？」

艾琳：「噢，沒有，我覺得將自己的照片放在網路上讓大家觀賞加評論，不是很聰明的做法。

老闆：「如果是這樣的話，我想妳可能太老而無法在這兒工作。」

艾琳：「等一下！你剛才不是才說我可以明天開始工作嗎？」

老闆：「不好意思，我改變了主意，不過我懷疑妳是否能夠和其他充滿活力的年輕員工合得來。」

艾琳：「但是……」

四、字彙庫 Word Bank

download [`daʊnˌlod] *v.*　　【電腦】下載

survive [sɚ`vaɪv] *v.*　　活下來，倖存

frankly [`fræŋklɪ] *adv.*　　坦率地說

privacy [`praɪvəsɪ] *n.*　　隱私

fit [fɪt] *v.*　　符合；配合

dynamic [daɪ`næmɪk] *a.*　　有活力的；有生氣的

staff [stæf] *n.*　　（全體）工作人員

Stay calm 抱持冷靜

　　發現職場上有人對你做出充滿歧視的批評，千萬要保持冷靜，不要火上加油，首先思考原因，先確定錯不在己，然後於必要時小心蒐集證據，投訴公司人力資源單位。

Seek help from professionals 求助於專業人士

　　歧視言語可能導致嚴重的霸凌行為，如果發現自己身心因此受到影響，則要馬上求助於心理諮商師等專業人士。

Consider leaving the job 考慮離職

　　職場上的各種歧視都很可能會干擾到正常的溝通與工作，引起不必要的爭執，並非所有相關的問題都可以輕易化解，必要時請衡量個人的利弊得失來決定去留。

Chapter

8

Negotiation

協商

一、簡介 Short Introduction

　　用英語協商的難度可以想見，因為即使對以英語為母語人士來說，也並非輕而易舉，因為這涉及談判技巧，需要累積相當的實戰經驗，才能完全掌握。本章依照談判要點，整理出最基礎的英語協商表達方式，希望對於剛接觸協商的讀者有幫助，讀者研讀的重點在於將協商策略牢記於心，例如避免人身攻擊的情緒性用語，並且以這些策略為主軸，自己發展出適合所面臨情境的英語說法，如此才能掌握本章精華，而不是拾人牙慧。

二、常用表達方式 Useful Expressions 40

這時該怎麼說？

Unit 1 Strategies of negotiation
協商策略

---

1. Examine the situation
檢視情形

例 Can you help me figure out what happened?"
您能幫我看看到底發生了什麼事嗎？

例 What seems to be the real problems?"
真正的問題可能是什麼？

例 What has brought about this problem?"
導致這個問題發生的原因為何？

例 How long has this situation been going on?"
這個狀況持續了多久？

---

2. No personal attacks
避免人身攻擊

避免左欄的人身攻擊話語；請使用右欄的非人身攻擊話語。

Personal attack 人身攻擊	No personal attack 避免人身攻擊
"What's the point talking to you now? You always change your mind at the last minute." 「現在跟你談這個有什麼用？你總是在最後一刻改變主意。」	"Maybe we should talk about the arrangement of the press conference now?" 「或許我們現在該來討論一下記者招待會的安排事項。」
"Don't tell me what to do all the time. You are not my boss!" 「不要老是告訴我該做什麼，你不是我的老闆！」	"Thank you for reminding me of my work. Now I know pretty well what I should do in the office." 「謝謝提醒我份內的工作，現在我很清楚我在辦公室該做的事。」
"You can never trust our CEO. He said he would give me a raise but it never happened." 「我們的執行長根本不值得信賴，他說要給我加薪，結果根本沒有。」	"I'm going to have a talk with our CEO about my raise. He seems to have forgotten it." 「我要跟我們執行長談加薪的事，他似乎已經忘了。」
"It's tough to work under a female manager. She seems to be in a bad mood again." 「女性經理真難共事，她好像又心情不好了。」	"Something seems to go wrong here. Our new manager looks very frustrated." 「這裡好像出了什麼事，我們的新經理看起十分沮喪。」
"The workers who go on strike are just too demanding. I have no sympathy for them." 「那些罷工的工人要求太多了，我對他們一點也不同情。」	"There must be ways to solve the problems of the workers who are having a strike." 「一定有什麼辦法可以解決罷工中的勞工的問題。」

3. Decipher emotions correctly
正確解讀感情

Misinterpret the emotions 錯誤解釋感情	Decipher emotions correctly 正確解讀感情
"Why are you getting so upset about this? If there is anyone who should get upset, it's me." 「為什麼你為此如此難過？該難過的人應該是我才對。」	"What is upsetting you now? Are you not happy about this assignment?" 「為什麼你這麼難過？你難道不喜歡這項任務嗎？」
"Why are you looking so serious? It is no big deal." 「為什麼你看起來如此嚴肅？又沒有什麼大不了的。」	"You look anxious. What's worrying you about this deal?" 「你看起來很焦慮，你覺得這項交易有什麼不妥的地方嗎？」
"Both of you seem to be quite happy about this agreement, right?" 「你們雙方似乎都對這協議感到很高興，是吧？」	"If either of you are not satisfied with this agreement, please feel free to let me know." 「如果你們當中任何一方對這協議有什麼不滿意之處，請讓我知道，不要客氣。」
"Don't overreact again! It's just a bit of extra work in the end of the year." 「不要又反應過度！這只不過是年底前的一點額外工作。」	"I'm sorry to give you extra workload. If you finish it in time, you can have two extra days off." 「不好意思給你增添工作，如果你能及時完成，就可以多放兩天的假。」

2 Prevention of future conflicts

避免未來的衝突

---

1. Make agreements for the future
為未來達成協議

例 The contract we had with this company has to be adjusted immediately.

我們和這家公司的合約需要馬上修改。

例 Next time we should think carefully before signing a contract with the city government.

下次我們應該要想清楚再和市政府簽合約。

例 Ask the Human Resources Manager to come up with a SOP to deal with cases like this.

請人力資源經理提出標準作業程序來處理類似像這樣的案例。

---

2. Develop strategies
研發策略

例 In the future, we will switch our supplier from company A to company B.

將來我們會將供應廠商由A公司轉為B公司。

例 Next time make sure we have all written agreements checked by our lawyers.

下次一定要請我們的律師檢查所有的書面協議書。

例 Since you are so good at negotiation, we'll send you to represent our company in the next meeting.
既然你對談判這麼在行，下場會議我們會派你代表公司參加。

---

3. Remember to ask yourself the following questions
記得問自己以下的問題

例 What are the real issues underneath the conflict?
這場衝突背後的真正問題為何？

例 How can I solve the conflicts effectively?
我該如何有效解決這些衝突？

例 What can be done to prevent future similar conflicts?
該如何避免未來發生類似衝突？

Unit 3 Mediation

調解

---

1. Listen to both sides of the story
聽兩方面的説法

例 Can any of you tell me how it all started?
你們有誰可以告訴我這是怎麼發生的

例 What made you so angry at each other?
你們為什麼會對彼此會這麼生氣？

例 Is there anything wrong with your contract?
你們的合約出了什麼問題嗎？

例 What are the real problems between you two?
你們倆之間的真正問題為何？

---

2. Help make an agreement
協助達成協議

例 What about making new schedule for this project?
要不要為這個專案規劃個新進度表？

例 How about arranging a meeting to negotiate with them again?
要不要再安排一場會議來和他們談判？

例 Why don't you make a new offer?
你何不提個新報價？

3. Prevent future conflicts
避免未來的衝突

例 Both of you would benefit from a new agreement.
你們倆都會從這個新協定中獲得好處。

例 Please let each other know if there is any change to the new agreement.
如果新協定有任何的改變，請讓彼此知道。

例 Follow this new agreement and you would not have similar problems.
遵循這個新協定你就不會有類似的問題。

三、情境對話 Situational Conversations

Ⓐ "What's the matter with you, Jason? You've been late three times and never spoken up in recent meetings."

Ⓑ "Sorry about that. Two weeks ago I just moved to a new place with my big family."

Ⓐ "Have you settled down finally?"

B "And a week ago my old mother fell down in the bathroom and is now in the hospital."

A "Sorry to hear about that, but you know the success of this project depends on the contribution of every team member."

B "As a matter of fact, I'd like to apply for deferred holidays from this Wednesday to Friday. Is it possible?"

A "Certainly you are aware we have to hand in the project in 17 days, and we are way behind our schedule. I understand you are having a tough time, but we have our deadline to meet."

B "During my days off, I'll be working on the project as well and reporting to you and other team members constantly."

A "Let me think about it... This is the first time you've asked to work from home..."

B "To be exact, I'll be working from hospital, taking care of my mother."

A "All right. Make sure you do show up in the office next Monday then."

B "I will."

A "Take a break this weekend and recharge yourself."

Ⓐ 「傑森，你怎麼了？你已經是第三次遲到，而且你在最近開會時都不曾發言。」

Ⓑ 「不好意思，兩星期前我剛和我的大家庭搬家到一個新房子。」

Ⓐ 「所以你已都安頓好了嗎？」

Ⓑ 「一星期前我的年邁母親在廁所跌倒，現在住院當中。」

Ⓐ 「真令人感到遺憾，但是你明白這個專案的成功要靠每位團隊成員的貢獻。」

Ⓑ 「事實上，這個星期三到星期五我想要申請補假，可以嗎？」

Ⓐ 「你非常清楚再過十七天我們就要交這個專案，而我們進度嚴重落後，雖然我明白你處境困難，但是我們要趕在截止日期前交件。」

Ⓑ 「在休假期間我也會繼續工作，並且經常向你與其他團隊成員報告。」

Ⓐ 「讓我想想看……這是你第一次要求在家工作……」

Ⓑ 「確切來說，我會在醫院一邊工作，一邊照顧我的母親。」

Ⓐ 「好吧，下星期一可要出現於辦公室喔。」

Ⓑ 「我會的。」

Ⓐ 「這個周末好好休息，充電一下。」

四、字彙庫 Word Bank

settle [`sɛt!] *v.*	安頓;安排
project [`pradʒɛkt] *n.*	方案,計畫,企劃
contribution [ˌkantrə`bjuʃən] *n.*	貢獻
defer [dɪ`fɝ] *v.*	推遲,延期
tough [tʌf] *a.*	艱困的,棘手的
deadline [`dɛdˌlaɪn] *n.*	截止期限,最後限期
recharge [ri`tʃardʒ] *v.*	再充電於

Be sincere 表示出誠意

　　無論發生什麼事，都要表現出願意溝通的誠意，相信協商的可能性，並且給予對方轉圜的餘地，這樣的態度也會感染給對方，增進彼此談判的成功率。

Listen carefully 仔細聆聽

　　或許對方情緒激動，甚至人身攻擊，但是如果我們專注聽他們真正想要表達的訊息，然後分析其用意與目的，就不難明瞭問題的關鍵所在；但是，倘若我們的情緒也隨著對方的音調提高而失控，那麼這場協商的失敗率就大大提高了。

Put yourself in the shoes of the other 站在對方立場看事情

　　如果能夠真正以對方的角度來看事情，協商的溝通也就成功了一大半，因為很多衝突就是因為雙方都沒有試著改變立場來看待問題，彼此互不讓步而造成的。

Chapter 9

9

Formal Business Meeting
正式商務會議

一、簡介 Short Introduction

在一場英語正式商務會議上，萬一就是怎麼也想不出某個重要英語字彙，怎麼樣也無法進入用英語發言的狀況，那該有多糗呢？但是如果這時將腦海中的景象飆換成為：你以優美的英語，語調不急不緩，從容不迫，堅定表達公司的立場，用字措辭之準確，令所有與會人士都留下深刻的印象，並且讚口不絕，會後都主動上前來與你交換名片，那該有多好！其實只要平時多練功，這一點也不難做到，以下就是正式商務會議上常見的英語慣用法總整理，多聽多練，你也可以成為代表公司參加正式會議的最佳人選。

二、常用表達方式 Useful Expressions 42

這時該怎麼說？

Unit

1 Opening the Meeting

開始會議

1. The opening
開場白

Ladies and gentlemen, it is my pleasure to be with you here today to...
各位先生女士，今天很榮幸能在這裡與您……

例 Ladies and gentlemen, it is my pleasure and honor to be with you here today to discuss how to save energy in the office building.
各位先生女士，今天很榮幸能在這裡與您討論在辦公室該如何節約能源。

2. The purpose of the meeting
會議主旨

Hello, everyone, I call this meeting to...
大家好，我召開這場會議來……

例 Hello, everyone, I call this meeting today to talk about how to generate more profits.
大家好，我召開這場會議來討論如何增加獲利。

3. Encourage participation and discussion
鼓勵大家參與討論

例 We welcome all opinions from all members who attend the meeting.
我們歡迎所有參與這場會議者的意見。

例 Let's brainstorm together during this meeting.
讓我們在這場會議中一起來腦力激盪一下。

例 The more you put in the meeting, the more you can get out of it.
您對這場會議付出的越多，得到的也就越多。

Unit
2 **Proceeding the Meeting**　　　　🅼🅿🅴 43

進行會議

1. Introducing the main purpose
介紹主要目的

Let's talk about the agenda...
讓我們來討論這個主題……

例 Let's talk about the agenda of this meeting, which is how to attract more clients.
我們來討論這場會議的主題，也就是吸引更多客戶的方法。

2. Call an intermission
中途休會

Let's take a short break...
讓我們中間休息一下……

例 Let's take a short break of 20 minutes and start the meeting again at 14:30.
讓我們休息二十分鐘，等到14:30再開會。

3. Postpone the meeting for a certain time
延至一段時間後再討論

I suggest that we postpone the discussion until...
我建議將討論延到……

例 I suggest that we postpone the discussion until 4 o'clock in the afternoon.
我建議下午四點後再討論。

例 I suggest postponing the meeting until tomorrow.
我建議將會議延到明天。

Can we postpone the meeting...
我們能不能將會議延後……

例 Can we postpone our meeting until tomorrow?
我們能不能將會議延到明天？

4. End debate
結束辯論

I suggest that we close the debate...
我建議結束辯論……

例 I suggest that we end this debate and start a new discussion.

我建議結束這場辯論，開始新的討論。

5. Change the wording of a motion (or amendment)
改變提議（或修正草案）的用字

I suggest that we amend the motion...
我建議修正這項提議……

例 I suggest that we amend the motion by adding this clause.

我建議在這項提議加上這修正條款。

6. Postpone the meeting indefinitely
永久延後會議

I suggest that we postpone this meeting indefinitely.
我建議將會議無限期延期。

例 If nobody wants to add something, I suggest that we postpone this meeting indefinitely.

如果沒有人要再提出什麼意見，我建議將會議無限期延期。

7. Set time for next meetings
設定下次開會的時間

I suggest that we meet again at... (time, place)
我建議我們於【時間】【地點】再會面。

例 I suggest that we meet again at 15:00 on 31 Oct. 2016.

我建議我們於 2016 年 10 月 31 日下午三點再會面。

8. Adjourn the meeting
休會

I suggest that we adjourn...
我建議休會……

例 I suggest that we now adjourn the meeting to a later date.

我建議現在休會，以後再召開會議。

MP3 44

Unit 3 Closing the Meeting

結束會議

1. Make a conclusion
做個總結

Let me summarize...   讓我總結一下……

例 Let me summarize our conclusions in this meeting.
讓我總結一下這場會議的結論。

**Let me recap (recapitulate)...
讓我重述一下重點……**

例 Let me recap (recapitulate) what we agreed on during this meeting.
讓我把我們在這場會議中所同意的重點重述一次。

2. End with encouragement for future cooperation
結束時以鼓勵話語為未來合作加油

例 After the meeting, I'm sure both of us know more about what we can achieve together than before.

在這場會議之後，我相信大家都比從前更明白共同合作能達成的結果。

例 Now that we've talked about our visions, I'm sure we can cooperate with each other seamlessly.

既然我們已經討論了彼此的願景，我相信我們一定能夠合作無間。

三、情境對話 Situational Conversations

Ⓐ "Good morning. I called this meeting to discuss how to promote our new products. Who would like to contribute to this topic first?"

Ⓑ "Why don't we put on an advertisement in all major newspapers?"

Ⓒ "That's right. We should hire models to wear our new sports outfits and show their photos in various media."

Ⓐ "Do you know any good places to sell our new sports products?"

Ⓑ "What about sports retail shops in gyms? Maybe we should give them some free samples for their customers to try out."

Ⓒ "How about selling our latest products online and on TV?"

Ⓐ "I'll give each of you some budgets to carry out the promotion plans. Do not overspend the budget and record the sales performances. It would be great if you two can brainstorm in designing the marketing campaign for the new products of this season."

Ⓐ 「早安！我決定召開這場會議來討論如何促銷我們的新產品，誰想要先針對這個主題發言？」

Ⓑ 「我們何不在所有大報上登廣告？」

Ⓒ 「對啊，我們應該雇模特兒穿我們的新款運動裝，然後在各種媒體展示模特兒照片。」

Ⓐ 「你知道有什麼好地方可以銷售我們的新款運動產品嗎？」

Ⓑ 「健身中心的運動零售店如何？或許我們應給他們一些免費的樣品，好給他們的顧客試用。」

Ⓒ 「要不要在網路和電視上賣我們的最新產品？」

Ⓐ 「我會各給你們一些預算來推動這個促銷計劃，不要超出預算，將銷售業績紀錄下來，如果你們兩個能夠一起腦力激盪來為這一季的新產品設計行銷活動，結果應該會很不錯。」

四、字彙庫 Word Bank

promote [prə`mot] *v.*	宣傳，推銷（商品等）
contribute [kən`trɪbjut] *v.*	貢獻
advertisement [ˌædvɚ`taɪzmənt] *n.*	廣告，宣傳
retail [`ritel] *n.*	零售
sample [`sæmp!] *n.*	樣品；試用品
budget [`bʌdʒɪt] *n.*	預算；經費
brainstorm [`brenˌstɔrm] *v.*	集體研討；集思廣益
campaign [kæm`pen] *n.*	運動，活動

貼 心 小 叮 嚀

Politeness and patience 有禮且耐心

　　無論與來自任何國家來的人進行商務往來，如果能夠全程抱持有禮貌的態度，對瑣碎的細節都充滿耐心，冷靜應對，那麼就非常可能達到目標，談成生意。

The control of timing 時間控制

　　合宜的時間控制能夠讓彼此都感到自在，增加會談的效果，當然這一點與各商務人士所來自的不同文化背景也息息相關，一般說來，美國人較重視時效，而中南美洲與亞洲人較願意花時間來社交，只要能將時間控制得讓賓主盡歡，也就更可能達成會議的共識。

Chapter

10

Signing a Contract

簽訂合約

一、簡介 Short Introduction

　　總算到了要簽訂合約的時候了，但是，可千萬不要以為一切已經大功告成，只要簽上大名即可，為了保障自我權益，簽訂合約過程還需要注意不少細節，倘若稍不注意，就驗證了所謂「魔鬼藏在細節裡」這句名言。本章的編排以簽訂合約的注意事項為骨幹，列出於此情形下會用到的英語常用說法，但是戲法人人會變，巧妙各有不同，還望讀者多加揣摩，靈活運用。

二、常用表達方式 Useful Expressions 45

這時該怎麼說？

1 What should you do before signing a contract?

在簽合約前應該做什麼？

---

1. Make sure the contract clearly states the rights and duties of both parties
確定合約明確記載雙方的權利與義務

☞ First of all, we should make sure the rights and duties of both parties are clearly stated in the contract.
首先我們該確定一下合約上清楚記載了雙方的權利與義務。

---

2. Check what remedies the contract contains for breach of the contract
確定合約上對於不履行合約的補償

☞ If they fail to deliver the products by 31st of October 2016, what action should we take?

如果他們在 2016 年十月 31 日前無法將貨送到，我們該採取什麼樣的行動？

3. Specify how disputes will be resolved
確定糾紛的解決方法

☞ In the contract, they have lawyers representing their company to deal with this.

在合約上寫著他們會請代表他們公司的律師來處理這件事。

4. Consider consequential damages
考慮可能的損失

☞ If the supplier cannot deliver their goods by the end of November, we will miss the Christmas sale.

如果供應廠商無法在十一月底前交貨，我們就會錯過了聖誕節拍賣。

5. Have a lawyer review the contract
請律師檢查合約

☞ To be on the safe side, please have our lawyer double check the contract they offered.
為了安全起見，請讓我們的律師再檢查一下他們提供的合約。

6. Check if they have references
看看對方是否有推薦者

☞ Who are your references?
你們有誰可以當推薦人嗎？

7. Ask if you can take the contract home and study it
詢問是否可以將合約帶回去研究

☞ May I have a copy of the contract?
可以給我一份合約嗎？

8. Make sure of the latest time to reply it
確認回覆的最後期限

☞ When should I give you my answer?
我最遲什麼時候必須要回覆？

2 Discussing a contract

🎧 46

討論合約

---

1. Confirm the dates and the amount of money
確定日期和金額

☞ Please take a close look at the deadline of delivery and the amount of fees.

請仔細看交貨的最遲日期和費用金額。

---

2. Discuss the specific details
討論特定細節

☞ Could you state the due date of payment in the contract?

請您在合約上明載付費的最遲日期好嗎？

---

3. Make sure the contract you sign is the one you read before
確定你簽的合約是之前看過的

☞ Let me quickly read through this contract before I sign it.
在簽名前，讓我很快再看一次這份合約。

4. Make sure the two contracts for both parties are identical
確定雙方的兩份合約完全相同

☞ Please put down your signatures on these two identical contacts, one for your company and one for us.
請在這兩份完全相同的合約上簽名，一份給你們公司，一份給我們。

5. Usually the host asks the guest sign first
通常主人會請客人先簽

☞ If there are no further questions, please sign your name on the dotted line here.
如果沒有其它問題，請在這裡的虛線上簽名。

Unit
3 **After signing a contract**

MP3 47

簽名後

1. Make a conclusion
總結

☞ Now that you've signed the contract, we will be looking forward to your delivery of the products.
既然您已經簽了合約，我們就等您出貨了。

2. End with encouragement for future cooperation
以鼓勵話語為未來合作加油

☞ Thank you for signing this contract with us, and we are sure there will be more opportunities of cooperation in the future.
謝謝您與我們簽約，相信未來我們會有更多的合作機會。

三、情境對話 Situational Conversations

A "Now that we've discussed almost everything about this project, it's time to seal this deal." (passing the contract over)

B "Yes, I'm ready to represent our company to sign the contract. Let me take a close look..."

A "Is there anything that we should adjust in the contract?"

B "This Article 7.2 really concerns me. Is it possible if we add a non-disclosure agreement to protect our new invention?"

A "As far as I understand, you are in the process of applying for a patent for this invention, but we can add a non-disclosure agreement for that to this contract, of course."

B "Thank you very much. That would really be of great help to us."

A "Aside from that, is there anything in the contract that is not clear to you?"

B "Not really. They are pretty much about everything we talked about before."

Ⓐ "If that's the case, please sign your name on the dotted line here."

Ⓑ "No problem."

Ⓐ 「既然我們已經討論了幾乎所有關於這專案的事項，現在該是簽下這筆交易的時候了。」（將合約傳過來）

Ⓑ 「好的，我準備好代表我們公司簽合約了。讓我仔細看一看……」

Ⓐ 「這份合約中有什麼我們需要修改的地方嗎？」

Ⓑ 「我覺得第7.2條不太妥當，我們是否可以加上保密協定來保護我們的新發明？」

Ⓐ 「就我所知，你們正在申請這項發明的專利，不過，我們當然可以於這合約上增加保密協定。」

Ⓑ 「非常謝謝你，這樣對我們會有很大的幫助。」

Ⓐ 「除此之外，這份合約上還有什麼你們不太清楚的嗎？」

Ⓑ 「沒有，幾乎都是我們之前談過的內容。」

Ⓐ 「既然如此，請在這裡的虛線上方簽名。」

Ⓑ 「沒問題。」

四、字彙庫 Word Bank

seal [sil] *v.*	保證；確認；批准
deal [dil] *n.*	交易
represent [ˌrɛprɪˈzɛnt] *v.*	代表
adjust [əˈdʒʌst] *v.*	調整
article [ˈɑrtɪk!] *n.*	條款，條文
concern [kənˈsɜ·n] *v.*	使擔心；使不安
disclosure [dɪsˈkloʒɚ] *n.*	揭發；透露；公開
non-disclosure agreement =	保密協定
patent [ˈpætnt] *n.*	專利；專利權
dotted [ˈdɑtɪd] *a.*	虛線的

貼心小叮嚀

Do some research about their reputation 打聽對方名聲

　　如果對方聲譽良好，與對方簽合約就較有保障，而這一點只有靠多方打聽才會知道。

Take the contract home to sign and send it by post later 將合約帶回家簽，然後再寄回

　　要求將合約帶回家，仔細研究後再簽，或是請別人幫忙檢查是否有問題，然後再郵寄給對方，這樣可以避免當場馬上簽合約可能會忽略的問題。

Chapter

11

Sales Language

銷售用語

一、簡介 Short Introduction

　　公司內所有工作人員都可能有機會需要介紹自家產品，特別是業務或接待人員，國際客戶詢問方式不僅只於電子郵件，也很可能在電話或商展上表達購買意願，因此平常就要熟悉銷售方面的英語口語表達方式，才不致於臨時亂了手腳。

二、常用表達方式 Useful Expressions

1. 討論價格：詢價、報價、議價

詢價

這時該怎麼問？

☞ Would you please give me a price quotation?
您可以給我報個價嗎？

☞ I'm interested to find out your lowest price quotation.
我對於貴公司的最低報價很感興趣。

☞ Would you mind sending me your latest price list?
您是否可以寄貴公司的價格表給我？

☞ May I take this catalog with me?
我可以將這份型錄帶走嗎？

☞ When are you going to have a special promotion?
貴公司何時會有特別的促銷呢？

報價

 這時該怎麼答？

☞ This product costs 500 Taiwan Dollars each.
這個產品一個要價台幣五百元。

☞ We charge 500 Taiwan Dollars for this item.
我們這個產品一個要價台幣五百元。

☞ The price range is from 300 to 600 Taiwan Dollars.
價格範圍在台幣三百到六百之間。

☞ The price of this product ranges from 300 to 600 Taiwan Dollars.
這個產品的價格在台幣三百到六百之間。

☞ This is our rock bottom price.
這是我們的最低價。

議價

 如何討價還價？

☞ How about giving us some special discounts?
可不可以給我們一點特別的優惠呢？

☞ Do you offer any discount for quantity buying?
大量購買是否有價格折扣呢？

☞ Could you give us a 10 percent discount if we buy more than 20 items?
如果我們買超過二十件，可以打九折嗎？

☞ Is there a discount if we pay cash?
如果我們付現金，可以算便宜點嗎？

☞ Do you know that another supplier charge us a lot less than you?
您知道其它供應商給我們的價格比你們低很多嗎？

 同意

☞ I can accept that price.
我可以接受那個價錢。

☞ I'll agree to that discounted price.
我可以同意那個打折後的價錢。

☞ We agree to give you 10 percent discount this time.
我方同意這次給您九折的優惠價。

☞ Since you agree to buy 100 items, I can offer you 10 percent discount.
既然您同意買一百個產品，我可以給您九折的優惠價。

☞ All right, but that is the lowest price we can go with.
好吧，不過那是我們能接受的最低價格。

不同意

☞ 10 percent discount is a bit too much. How about 5 percent discount?
九折有點太多了，九五折如何？

☞ We cannot make any profit if we accept that price.
如果我們接受那個價格就沒有任何利潤可賺了。

☞ I'm afraid that is the best price we can offer.
恐怕那就是我們可以提供的最低價格。

☞ Let me remind you our price is way below market value.
請容我提醒您，我們的價格遠比市價低。

☞ Sorry, no bargaining in this company.
不好意思，我們公司不二價。

2. 推銷用語（語氣由最弱到最強而排列）

1. Have you heard about our latest products?
您聽過我們的最新產品嗎？

2. Have you thought about using our latest products?
您想過要使用我們的最新產品嗎？

3. Would you mind taking a look at our latest products?
您要不要看看我們的最新產品？

4. Would you please take a look at our latest products?
請看看我們的最新產品好嗎？

5. Would you be willing to try our latest products?
   您願意試用我們的最新產品嗎？

6. Let me tell you about the features of our latest products.
   讓我告訴您我們最新產品的特色。

7. Wouldn't you want to try out our samples of the latest products?
   您是否想要試試我們的最新產品？

8. Haven't you thought about giving our latest products a try?
   您是否想過要改用我們的最新產品？

9. You'll save a lot energy and money if you use our latest products.
   您如果使用我們的最新產品就可節省很多能源與金錢。

10. You wouldn't want to miss our latest products.
    您絕對不會想錯過我們的最新產品。

11. You won't find any other products better than ours.
    您不會找到比我們更好的產品。

12. I guarantee that you will find that our latest products are the best in the market.
    我保證您會發現我們的最新產品在市場上排名第一。

3. 下訂單＆接訂單

 49

下訂單 Place an order

☞ We're ready to place our order now.
現在我們準備好要下訂單了。

☞ Will that necklace be in stock very soon?
那款項鍊很快就會有貨嗎？

☞ Will that item be back in stock before Christmas?
聖誕節前那件商品會再有貨嗎？

☞ I'll look at the catalog closely and place an order with you later.
我會好好研究型錄然後再向您下訂單。

☞ When can you ship it if I place an order with you right now?
如果我現在向您下訂單，何時可以送貨過來呢？

☞ What quantity do I have to purchase to have a discount?
我需要買多少數量才能有價格優惠呢？

接訂單 Accept an order

☞ Have you decided to place your order now?
您決定好現在要下訂單了嗎？

☞ That item is in stock at the moment.
那件商品現在有貨。

☞ That necklace is not in stock right now.
那款項鍊現在缺貨。

☞ That book is out of stock now.
那本書現在缺貨。

☞ Thank you very much for your order.
謝謝您向我們訂貨。

☞ Today is the last day for this special discount.
今天是這個特別折扣優惠的最後一天。

三、情境對話 Situational Conversations

(1)

A "We'd like to order 200 teddy bears of this size from you."

B "Great! Would you like to pay by cash or credit card?"

A "Is there any discount if I pay by cash upon receiving the toys?"

B "How about I give you 20% off?"

A "That's very nice of you."

B "The teddy bears will be sent to you by the day after tomorrow."

Ⓐ 「我們想要向您訂兩百隻這樣大小的泰迪熊。」

Ⓑ 「太好了！您想要付現還是刷卡？」

Ⓐ 「如果我收到這些玩具時付您現金，可以享有折扣嗎？」

Ⓑ 「我給您打八折怎麼樣？」

Ⓐ 「您真好心。」

Ⓑ 「後天前泰迪熊就會送達您那邊。」

(2)

Ⓐ "Hello, this is Kelly Chang, the coordinator of the Taipei International Book Exhibition. May I speak to your sales manager, Mr. Anderson?"

Ⓑ "Speaking."

Ⓐ "How have you been?"

Ⓑ "Pretty good. How can I help you?"

Ⓐ "Have you read the e-mail I sent you last week?"

Ⓑ "Yes, but I'm sorry haven't got the time to reply. It was about Paul Cleave's "Collecting Cooper", right?"

Ⓐ "Yes, we'd like to know if you could offer us a special discount if we order 200 copies."

Ⓑ　"Sure, we are glad to give you 15% off."

Ⓐ　"Thank you very much. What's more, is it possible for the books to arrive in Taipei by Feb. 10th?"

Ⓑ　"No problem."

Ⓐ 「哈囉，這裡是台北國際書展聯絡人張凱莉，我想與貴公司的銷售經理安德森先生説話。」

Ⓑ 「我就是。」

Ⓐ 「您好嗎？」

Ⓑ 「很好。請問有什麼需要我服務的嗎？」

Ⓐ 「請問您是否讀了上星期我寄給您的電子郵件？」

Ⓑ 「我讀了，不過真不好意思，我至今沒時間回覆，是關於保羅・克里夫的《殺手收藏家》，是吧？」

Ⓐ 「是的，我們想知道如果訂兩百本，是否可以享有優惠價。」

Ⓑ 「當然可以，我們很樂意給您打八五折。」

Ⓐ 「非常感謝您。還有，這些書是否可以在二月十日前送達台北呢？」

Ⓑ 「沒問題。」

四、字彙庫 Word Bank

quotation [kwoˋteʃən] *n.*	報價
catalog [ˋkætəlɔg] *n.*	型錄
promotion [prəˋmoʃən] *n.*	促銷
range [rendʒ] *n. v.*	範圍
bargain [ˋbɑrgɪn] *v.*	討價還價
stock [stɑk] *n.*	存貨
feature [fitʃɚ] *n.*	特色
sample [ˋsæmp!] *n.*	樣品
guarantee [ˌgærənˋti] *v.*	保證
quantity [ˋkwɑntətɪ] *n.*	數量

貼心小叮嚀

Zone of possible agreement 議價空間

　　事前先做足功課，找出該公司可能願意成交的最低價，並研究市場以找出你願意出的最高價，這兩者之間即是議價空間，談判時就是要不斷將價錢推向最低價，同時要注意對方所提出的交易條件，例如零利率分期付款與保固期等等，整體衡量後做出是否與對方達成交易的決定。

Bargaining chips 談判籌碼

　　有時候交易現場會出現類似拍賣會的情形，像近年來有些房地產的買賣與租賃就是如此，多個買家必須要向賣家出價，一起來競標，這時就更要強調自己的談判籌碼，例如付款方式，以及過去成功例子、將來發展方案等等，這些都可以為得標大大加分。

Chapter ⑫

Payment Terms

付款方式

一、簡介 Short Introduction

 50

在國際貿易上付款多半使用下列三個方式：

(1) L/C (Letter of Credit) 信用狀付款

(2) D/P (Documents against Payment) 付款交單：買方必須先付清託收匯票貸款，才能取得貨運單據，辦理提貨。

(3) D/A (Documents against Acceptance) 承兌交單：買方必須於賣方開製的託收匯票，簽名承認到期付款，才能取單提貨。

這三種付款條件，對出口商的保障優劣依序為 (1) L/C 大於 (2) D/P 大於 (3)D/A

二、常用表達方式 Useful Expressions

☞ What are your payment terms?
請問貴公司的付款條件為何？

☞ Are you planning to pay by cash or check?
您計劃要付現金還是支票？

☞ We prefer you to open a letter of credit to pay for this order.
我們比較想要您開信用狀來付這訂單的費用。

☞ Is it possible if we pay a 30% down payment?
我們付百分之三十的頭期付款可以嗎？

☞ Do you accept payment by installments?
您接受分期付款嗎？

☞ I was wondering if you would accept payment terms such as D/P or D/A?
不知道您接受付款交單或承兌交單的付款條件嗎？

☞ Please extend the validity of this L/C to March 1st.
請將這信用狀的有效期限延長至三月一日。

☞ We only accept D/A under special circumstances.
只有在特殊情形下我們才接受承兌交單。

☞ We'll agree to D/A this time to save time.
為了節省時間，這次我們接受承兌交單。

☞ In what currency should we make payment?
我們該用什麼貨幣來付款呢？

三、情境對話 Situational Conversations

(1)

Ⓐ "What are your payment terms?"

Ⓑ "We accept letter of credit only."

Ⓐ "When would you like me to open a L/C?"

Ⓑ "Any time that suits you."

Ⓐ 「請問貴公司的付款條件為何？」

Ⓑ 「我們只接受信用狀。」

Ⓐ 「請問您希望我什麼時候開信用狀？」

Ⓑ 「只要您方便，任何時候都可以。」

(2)

Ⓐ "We would like to suggest a 10% down payment."

Ⓑ "It is our usual practice to have a 30% down payment."

Ⓐ "Can't you be a bit flexible this time?"

Ⓑ "All right, 20% then."

Ⓐ 「我們建議付百分之十的頭期付款。」

Ⓑ 「我們通常要求百分之三十的頭期付款。」

Ⓐ 「這次您可以有點彈性嗎？」

Ⓑ 「好吧，那麼就百分之二十吧。」

(3)

Ⓐ "Do you accept D/P or D/A?"

Ⓑ "Yes, but only when you order large quantities of goods."

Ⓐ "I see. I'll talk to my boss about that and get back to you."

Ⓑ "Thank you very much."

Ⓐ 「請問您接受付款交單或承兌交單嗎？」

Ⓑ 「接受，不過只有在訂貨量很大的時候。」

Ⓐ 「我明白了。我會轉告我的老闆，然後再回覆您。」

Ⓑ 「多謝了。」

(4)

Ⓐ "Your payment is long overdue again."

Ⓑ "Sorry. Please give us a bit more time."

Ⓐ "We'll have to put you on Cash on Delivery."

Ⓑ "Please don't do that."

Ⓐ「您的款項又逾期很久未付了。」

Ⓑ「抱歉，請再多給我們一些時間。」

Ⓐ「我們只好將貴公司改為貨到付款。」

Ⓑ「請不要這樣。」

四、字彙庫 Word Bank

term [tɝm] *n.*	條件
installment [ɪn`stɔlmənt] *n.*	分期付款
validity [və`lɪdətɪ] *n.*	有效性
circumstance [`sɝkəm,stæns] *n.*	情況
currency [`kɝənsɪ] *n.*	貨幣
flexible [`flɛksəb!] *a.*	有彈性的
overdue [`ovɚ`dju] *a.*	逾期未付的
delivery [dɪ`lɪvərɪ] *n.*	交貨

D/A、D/P交易的優缺點：

國際貿易日益頻繁，買方市場日漸抬頭，非信用狀的付款方式越來越普遍，目前的趨勢為逐漸以付款交單（D/P）代替即期信用狀（Sight L/C）；以承兌交單（D/A）取代遠期信用狀（Usance L/C）。

D/A、D/P的優點：

以進口商而言：進口商若用D/A，D/P方式則不需要繳納保證金，只需繳部份手續費及電報費；貨物不符合契約條件時，可拒絕付款。

D/A、D/P的缺點：

以出口商而言：出口商必需承擔客戶到期延遲付款或不付款的風險，不像信用狀交易付款那樣有保障。

Chapter 13

Packing, Shipment & Insurance

包裝、裝運及保險

一、簡介 Short Introduction 51

　　現今網路購物如此發達，無論是在國內或國外的網站上，似乎只要輕鬆按幾個按鍵，想要買的貨品在幾天內就會自動送到家門口了，但是，你知道這當中的包裝與裝運，究竟經過了多少複雜的過程嗎？就拿在外國網站買本英文小說送給朋友來說，就可以選擇是否要買精裝本，要買全新還是半新的書，是否要以禮物紙包裝，是否需要以空運加快遞方式寄達，寄達時間甚至還可以要求必須於聖誕節前，當然這些裝運費用並不便宜。現在，就讓我們來學習一些關於包裝、裝運及保險的英語用法，才不會出現時常感嘆「書到用時方恨少」的情形。

二、常用表達方式 Useful Expressions

1. Packing
包裝

例 Please pay attention to the packing instructions.
請注意包裝指示。

例 This order requires special packing.
這批貨需要特別的包裝。

例 Who should pay for the packing charge?
這包裝費該由誰來付呢？

例 We found damaged goods in this freight due to the poor packaging.
我們在這批貨物中發現受損的商品，是因為包裝不良引起的。

例 The packaging of this order has to be water-proof.
這批貨的包裝必須防水。

例 There is a SOP of the packing service for the famous paintings sold here.
這裡的名畫包裝服務有標準作業程序。

例 What sort of packing would you recommend for shipping these fragile cups?
您會怎麼建議裝運這些易碎的杯子？

例 You can package your items by yourself if there are not that many.
如果東西不會太多的話，您可以自行包裝。

2. Shipment
裝運

例 Please ship these products to the two different addresses.
請將這些產品裝運至這兩個不同的地址。

(例) We cannot guarantee all of the items could be shipped there by Christmas.

我們無法保證能將所有東西在聖誕節前寄達。

(例) Your goods should be able to arrive in China by the Lunar New Year.

您的商品應該能在農曆新年前送達中國。

(例) I'd like to designate Kaohsiung as the loading port and Hamburg as the unloading port.

我想要指定高雄作為起運港，漢堡作為卸貨港。

(例) We recommend sea mail if you would like to send a large number of old books.

如果您想寄大量舊書，我們推薦用海運寄。

(例) How much would it cost me if I want to send it the fastest way to the States?

用最快方式寄到美國，需要多少費用？

(例) Which shipping company would you recommend if I want to ship fruit to Beijing?

如果我要裝運水果到北京，您會推薦哪家貨運公司呢？

(例) You can pay 50% before shipment and 50% upon receiving the goods.

您可以出貨前付五成，收到貨馬上付清尾款。

(例) During shipping all of the fruit has to be kept at a very low temperature.

在運送過程中所有的水果都需要保持於極低溫度。

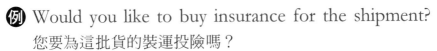

3. Insurance
保險

MP3 52

例 Would you like to buy insurance for the shipment?
您要為這批貨的裝運投險嗎？

例 Do I really need insurance for this shipping?
我真的需要為這次裝運投保嗎？

例 "This insurance provides cover for damage to or loss of the goods.
這保險會提供這些貨品損壞及遺失的理賠。

例 What types of insurance is suitable to me this time?
這次投保哪些險才適合我呢？

例 Most people purchase this insurance against theft when they send jewelry.
大部分人在寄珠寶時會加保竊盜險。

例 In our shipping company, the insurance is included in the shipping fees.
在我們貨運公司，運費內包含保險。

例 Make sure your precious gift is properly insured with the shipping.
您一定要為珍貴禮物的裝運買足夠的保險。

例 If the item does not cost much, there is no need to purchase insurance.
如果這物品不會太昂貴，就沒有買保險的必要。

三、情境對話 Situational Conversations

(1)

A "How would you like to ship these boxes?"

B "These are boxes of books. It should be fine to send them via sea mail."

A "It will take 3 to 4 months for these boxes to arrive in the U.K."

B "That's all right."

A "Please weigh these boxes one by one."

B "Okay."

A 請問您要如何送這幾箱東西？

B 這些箱子裡面是書，用海運寄應該可以。

A 這些箱子寄到英國要三到四個月。

B 那可以。

A 請一一秤這些箱子。

B 好的。

(2)

Ⓐ "I'd like to send this parcel to my mother."

Ⓑ "What is inside of the parcel?"

Ⓐ "It is a silver necklace made by myself. It's a gift for my mother."

Ⓑ "Does that cost very much?"

Ⓐ "For me, it is priceless."

Ⓑ "In that case, I think you should insure your parcel against theft."

Ⓐ 我想要寄這個包裹給我母親。

Ⓑ 包裹裡面裝什麼？

Ⓐ 是一條我自己做的銀項鍊，是要給我母親的禮物。

Ⓑ 很貴重嗎？

Ⓐ 對我而言是無價之寶。

Ⓑ 那麼我認為您應該為包裹保竊盜險。

四、字彙庫 Word Bank

instruction [ɪn`strʌkʃən] *n.*	指示
package [`pækɪdʒ] *v.*	把……打包；包裝
freight [fret] *n.*	貨物；運費
SOP = standard operating procedure	標準作業程序
recommend [ˌrɛkə`mɛnd] *v.*	推薦
fragile [`frædʒəl] *a.*	易碎的
designate [`dɛzɪɡˌnet] *v.*	指定
load [lod] *v.*	裝貨
unload [ʌn`lod] *v.*	卸貨
priceless [`praɪslɪs] *a.*	無價的

注意裝運規定與保險

　　有些產品需要特殊的包裝方式，例如有的水果需要 0
－3度的超低溫以及保麗龍裝箱空運，這些都要明列清楚，
而出貨公司務必要按照包裝指示來打包裝箱，如此才能避
免日後可能發生的索賠問題；時效則是裝運的重大課題，
尤其是在農曆新年與聖誕節等重大送禮時節更形重要，因
此必須以白紙黑字明列細節於合約上；除此之外，加上必
要的保險可於未來發生意外狀況時，得以從容給付隨之而
來的理賠金額。

常見的包裝用語

This Side Up	此面朝上
Keep Dry	保持乾燥
Handle with Care	小心輕放
Keep Cool	保持冷藏
Fragile	易碎
Inflammable	易燃
Dangerous	危險
Poisonous	有毒

常見的裝貨保險用語

F.P.A. = Free of Particular Average	平安險
W.P.A. = With Particular Average	水漬險
T.P.N.D. = Theft, Pilferage and Non-Delivery	竊盜及不能送達險
S.R.C.C. = Strike, Riot and Civil Commotion	罷工、暴動和民眾騷擾險
T.L.O. = Total Loss Only	全損險
War Risk	兵險

Chapter 14

14

Claim & Arbitration
索賠及仲裁

一、簡介 Short Introduction

　　一般人都不希望於商業交易時發生需要論及索賠的情形，因為大家都明白和氣生財的道理，但是商場上往往人算不如天算，發生爭端的情形時有所聞，而且問題常關係著彼此的金錢利益與公司信譽，如果遇到對方得寸進尺，還是要請中立的仲裁人來協調，必要時採取法律途徑索賠，但是若是對方已經釋出善意願意和解，那麼還是要以和為貴，儘量爭取雙贏，以樹立企業於業界的優良名聲。有時突然遇到需要以英語來索賠或仲裁的情形，可能會一時不知該如何來表達，請參考以下這些常見用法，平時多做準備，才能於適當時機派上用場。

二、常用表達方式 Useful Expressions 53

1. Claim
索賠

遲到問題

例 What caused the delay of the freight?
這批貨為什麼耽擱了？

例 How long do I have to wait for the arrival of the goods?

我還要等多久，才能收到這些商品呢？

例 Could you ask the shipping company why this freight is late?

您可以問貨運公司這批貨為何遲到了嗎？

例 The shipment was delayed due to the strike of the workers at the airport.

貨運因為機場工作人員罷工而延誤了。

例 The books were sent on 1st of October by air mail and should arrive in the middle of October.

這些書本是在十月一日以空運寄出，應該於十月中會到達。

例 How are you going to make up for the late arrival of Valentine chocolates?

你們要如何彌補情人節巧克力太遲送達呢？

貨物問題

例 5 items seem to be missing among the products you sent to us.

您寄給我們的商品中似乎少了五件。

例 There seem to be some problems with the samples we just received.

我們剛收到的樣品似乎出了點問題。

例 Could you please replace the two broken pans with new ones?
有兩個鍋子壞了，您可以補新的給我們嗎？

例 The calendars you sent to us are not the type which I ordered.
您寄給我們的月曆並非是我訂的那一型。

例 There is a mistake with spelling on the pens.
這些筆上面的字拼錯了。

例 Is there anything you can do to send us the right goods as soon as possible?
您能儘速將正確的商品寄給我們嗎？

帳單問題

例 There is one huge mistake in the invoice.
出貨明細表上出了個大錯誤。

例 The invoice seems to be someone else's, not ours.
這出貨明細表似乎是別人的，不是我們的。

例 The total amount of the fees is not correct.
總共費用的金額不正確。

例 I believe we are overcharged for what we bought.
我想我們被多算了錢。

例 I'll ask our accountant to reply to you about this.
我會請我們會計回覆您這個問題。

例 We are sorry for not paying the bill on time again.
不好意思，我們再度遲繳費用。

例 I will have someone double check the bill and then pay the fees.

我會請人檢查帳單，然後去繳費。

例 Please let me know the extra charges of the shipping fee in advance next time.

下回請先讓我知道額外的運送費用。

2. Arbitration
仲裁

例 Arbitration is a process of settling a disagreement in which the people on both sides present their opinions to a third person."

仲裁是雙方人士將意見提供給第三者來裁決糾紛的過程。

例 I suggest that we consult an independent arbitrator to rule on this issue.

我建議將這個問題請中立的仲裁人來裁決。

例 We should have an authoritative third party as our arbitrator."

我們的仲裁人必須要是具權威的第三者。

例 Arbitration is the last resort to sort out an argument.

仲裁是解決爭論的最後途徑。

例 The arbitration fees should be paid by the losing party."

仲裁費用應該要由輸的那一方來支付。

例 In my opinion, we should sign an agreement with the presence of an arbitrator."

依我看來，我們應該要在仲裁人面前簽訂和解協議書。

例 Do you think arbitration can bring us advantages or disadvantages?"

您認為仲裁會帶給我們好處還是壞處？

例 When we present the case to the arbitrator, we should have all evidences ready."

我們要請仲裁人來處理這個案子時，必須要準備好所有證據。

三、情境對話 Situational Conversations MP3 54

(1)

Ⓐ "Almost all of these candles for Christmas sales season were broken when they arrived."

Ⓑ "We are terribly sorry, but it was the fault of the shipping company."

Ⓐ "Do you have any idea how much loss it caused us?"

Ⓑ "We have filed claim for the compensation. As soon as we hear anything, we'll let you know."

Ⓐ「幾乎所有聖誕節檔期的蠟燭在寄到時都已損壞了。」

Ⓑ「我們感到非常抱歉，不過這是貨運公司的錯。」

Ⓐ「您知道這對我們造成了多大的損失？」

Ⓑ「我們已經申請賠償，只要我們一有任何消息，就會馬上通知您。」

(2)

Ⓐ "So far this order has been delayed for more than two months."

Ⓑ "We checked with the shipping company, and it was confirmed that the order was sent on time and so far nothing has been returned."

Ⓐ "Due to that, we didn't have the products to display in the trade fair yesterday."

Ⓑ "According to our company policy, I'm afraid we cannot send you new products now."

Ⓐ "It seems to me that we need an independent arbitrator in this case."

Ⓑ "I regret what happened, and we will do all we can to cooperate with your company."

Ⓐ「這批貨至今已經耽擱了兩個月多。」

B「我們詢問了貨運公司，確認了這批貨是準時寄出的，至今並沒有被退回。」

A「因為這個緣故，我們昨天在商展上沒有商品可以展示。」

B「依我們公司政策的規定，我們現在恐怕無法送新產品給您。」

A「看來我們似乎需要一位中立的仲裁人來解決這個問題。」

B「對於已發生的事我感到很遺憾，我們將會竭盡所能配合貴公司。」

四、字彙庫 Word Bank

invoice [ˋɪnvɔɪs] *n.*	發貨清單，出貨文件
overcharge [ˋovəˋtʃɑrdʒ] *v.*	對……索價過高
arbitrator [ˋɑrbəˌtretə] *n.*	仲裁人
authoritative [əˋθɔrəˌtetɪv] *a.*	權威性的，可信賴的
compensation [ˌkɑmpənˋseʃən] *n.*	賠償
regret [rɪˋgrɛt] *v.*	因……而遺憾
cooperate [koˋɑpəˌret] *v.*	配合；合作

據理力爭

在合理範圍內向對方索賠，不但是自身的權利，也是對業界其他業者的保護，因此應當據理力爭，也可以向具公權力的單位申訴，例如消費者保護協會的消保官，這樣不但能自保也可以杜絕不肖廠商的不當營利行為。

和解協議書

在雙方已經達成和解之後，還需要到調解庭，在具公信力的仲裁人面前簽下和解協議書，例如債務和解協議書，這樣才可以避免將來某一方因後悔而產生的不必要問題。

Chapter
15

Agency

代理

一、簡介 Short Introduction

　　進口產品占台灣市場極大的比例，因此代理商之間的競爭非常激烈，英語是與大部分外國廠商溝通的基本工具，要如何才能於第一次接洽就用流利英語讓對方對你留下深刻印象，接著又要如何以英語表現出專業形象與服務態度，佐以豐富的成功代理經驗，最後讓對方願意放心將其產品交由你的公司來做獨家代理，於國內市場首次亮相，這些都是要做很多事前準備的。接下來的常用英語表達方式能於此助你一臂之力，要點還是要多加演練，以達到熟能生巧。

二、常用表達方式 Useful Expressions
MP3 55

1. The agent
代理商

例 We are very interested in acting as your sole agent in Taiwan.
敝公司想要擔任貴公司在台灣的獨家代理商。

例 We'd like to offer to be your exclusive agent for your chocolates in Taiwan.
敝公司想要擔任貴公司在台灣的巧克力獨家代理商。

例 We have years of experiences in representing mobile devices in Taiwan.

敝公司於台灣代理行動配備有多年的經驗。

例 We are the biggest copyrights agency in Taiwan.

敝公司為台灣最大家的著作版權代理公司。

例 We are interested in signing a sole agency agreement with you.

敝公司有意與貴公司簽訂獨家代理協議。

例 The commission we offer is very reasonable compared to others.

敝公司提供的佣金比起其它公司來說非常合理。

例 Our service as an agency is famous in this line of business.

敝公司提供的代理服務在業界非常出名。

例 Please consider our application for your sole agent seriously because we are particularly good at marketing sports products.

請慎重考慮我們申請擔任貴公司獨家代理商的計劃，因為我們特別擅長於行銷運動產品。

2. The principal
出口商、貨主

例 Thank you for your interest in being our exclusive agent."

感謝您有興趣成為敝公司的獨家代理商。

例 We'll consider your proposal of acting as our sole agent in Japan.
我們會考慮貴公司提議擔任我方於日本的獨家代理商的計劃。

例 We have appointed your company as our sole agent in the United States.
我們已指定貴公司為我方在美國的獨家代理商。

例 How many years of exclusive agency of our products are you thinking of?
貴公司想要獨家代理我方產品幾年？

例 Please tell me your experiences in acting as an agent for smart phones.
請告訴我貴公司代理智慧型手機的經驗。

例 We cannot accept your proposal because we have already appointed an agent in your country.
敝公司不能答應貴公司的提案，因為敝公司已經在貴國指定了代理商。

例 We do not think it is the right time to talk about appointing an agent abroad.
我們認為現在不是討論指定國外代理商的時機。

例 We'll inform you when we are ready to appoint an exclusive agent in your country.
我們要於貴國指定獨家代理商時便會通知貴公司。

3. Commission
佣金

例 What is your standard commission?
貴公司的佣金通常如何計算？

例 Could you lower your commission to 8%?
是否可以將你們佣金降到百分之八？

例 We are sorry, but this is our lowest commission.
不好意思，這是我們佣金的最低限度。

例 After I talk with my boss about the commission, I'll get back to you.
等我與我老闆討論佣金之後再回覆您。

例 This is our practice in commission to charge 10% for each piece.
我們通常的計算方式就是按每件價格抽百分之十當佣金。

例 Our commission depends on the quantity you purchase with us.
我們的佣金依您跟我們購買的數量來決定。

例 If you can pay cash right now, I can give you 10% off in the commission.
如果您可以馬上付現金的話，我可以給您佣金打九折。

例 If you order more than 1000 pieces, we can talk about reducing the commission.
如果您訂購的數量超過一千件，我們再來談佣金打折之事。

三、情境對話 Situational Conversations 56

(1)

Ⓐ "We'd like to be your exclusive agent in Japan."

Ⓑ "Are you specialized in garments? "

Ⓐ "Yes, and we are particularly interested in your children's clothes."

Ⓑ "Are you based in Japan?"

Ⓐ "Yes, and we sell our products to all retailers in almost all countries in Asia."

Ⓑ "In that case, maybe we can talk about the possibility of having you as our exclusive agent in the whole Asia."

Ⓐ 「我們想要成為貴公司在日本的獨家代理商。」

Ⓑ 「貴公司的強項是服裝嗎？」

Ⓐ 「是的，我們對貴公司的童裝特別感興趣。」

Ⓑ 「貴公司位於日本嗎？」

Ⓐ 「是的，我們合作的零售商幾乎遍及亞洲各國。」

Ⓑ 「這樣的話，或許我們可以來商量是否可以請貴公司來擔任我們在全亞洲的獨家代理商。」

(2)

Ⓐ "Do you have an agent in Taiwan?"

Ⓑ "Not yet. As you know, our company is rather new in Asia."

Ⓐ "Would you consider us to be your sole agent in Taiwan?"

Ⓑ "Thank you for your interest in us. Could you please send me some references first?"

Ⓐ "No problem. We are a successful jewelry company and have represented many European jewelry companies so far."

Ⓐ 「貴公司在台灣有代理商嗎？」

Ⓑ 「還沒有。如您所知，我們在亞洲算是相當新的公司。」

Ⓐ 「貴公司會考慮由我們來當在台灣的獨家代理商嗎？」

Ⓑ 「謝謝您對我們感興趣，可以請您先寄些推薦信給我好嗎？」

Ⓐ 「沒問題，我們是一家成功的珠寶行，至今代理了很多家歐洲珠寶公司。」

四、字彙庫 Word Bank

sole [sol] *a.*	唯一的
exclusive [ɪk`sklusɪv] *a.*	唯一的
represent [ˌrɛprɪ`zɛnt] *v.*	作為……的代表
copyright [`kɑpɪˌraɪt] *n.*	版權；著作權
reasonable [`riznəb!] *a.*	合理的
outstanding [`aʊt`stændɪŋ] *a.*	傑出的
principal [`prɪnsəp!] *n.*	出口商、貨主
commission [kə`mɪʃən] *n.*	佣金
garment [`gɑrmənt] *n.*	服裝
reference [`rɛfərəns] *n.*	推薦

貼 心 小 可 嚀

多方打聽信譽

　　想要代理某外國品牌前，可以利用當地公會來調查該公司的信譽，或是在業界多方打聽，當然也要衡量自家公司是否有相當的資格，能夠為對方所信賴，做足功課後才向對方提出代理意願。

避免雙重代理

　　如果發現某一外國品牌值得代理，一定要先於國內市場內徹底調查，看看是否有廠商已經獲得其獨家代理權，以避免將來發生雙重代理的法律糾紛。

Customer Service

客戶服務

一、簡介 Short Introduction

　　很多職場新鮮人最先都是由客服工作開始做起，千萬不要小看這樣的職位，這可是接觸顧客的第一線工作，影響到顧客對於企業服務品質的第一印象，也是很多顧客決定是否要購買的考量因素之一，因此是否能好好掌握這當中的訣竅，對於客服工作的績效影響極大。如果遇到需要用英語來做客服，並且與顧客達成交易，難度就又更高了，本章的內容就是針對此主題而撰寫的，除了一般的英語禮貌用語，還整理好英文中常用的客服句型，不僅可以幫助你與客戶的一般溝通，也可以讓說英語的顧客更加信賴你的專業能力，而成為常客並向朋友推薦你的服務。

二、 常用表達方式 Useful Expressions

① 30 phrases customers want to hear
　30 個顧客想聽到的片語

1. Welcome & the beginning of the service
歡迎＆服務開始

例 "Hello!／Hi!"
「哈囉／嗨！」
這是較為不正式的打招呼方式。

例 "Good morning/afternoon!"

「早安／午安！」

這是較為正式的打招呼方式，視顧客到來時間而變化。

例 "Welcome to 【　　】!"

「歡迎來到【　　】！」

歡迎顧客來到此店家，可以加深客人對店名的印象。

例 "Sir."

「先生」

不確定顧客的名字時，可用此來稱呼男性客人。

例 "Ma'am."

「女士」

不確定顧客的名字時，可用此來稱呼女性客人。

例 "Mr./Mrs./Ms. 【　　】."

「【　　】先生／太太／小姐」

如果知道對方姓名則可以稱呼對方為某某先生／太太／小姐，可視需要加上名字。

例 "Hi, Mr./Mrs. 【　　】. It's great to see you again."

「嗨！【　　】先生／女士，很高興再見到您。」

對方為熟人，則可以如此稱呼。

例 "I'm pleased to meet you."
「我很高興再見到您。」
當被介紹給顧客時，可以此作為開場白。

例 "My name is 【　　】."
「我叫【　】。」
視時機決定是否自我介紹。

例 "How can I help you?"
「有什麼需要我服務的嗎？」
詢問顧客是否需要幫忙的問話。

例 "What can I help you with today?"
「今天有什麼需要我服務的嗎？」
顧客很可能為熟客，此為詢問顧客今天需要什麼服務的問話。

例 "What can I do for you today?"
「今天有什麼我可以服務的嗎？」
顧客很可能為熟客，此為上一句更直接的問話。

例 "Are you looking for anything in particular?"
「你在找什麼特別的東西嗎？」
特別用在顧客在店家找尋合適商品的時候。

例 "Can I help you find something?"
「有什麼需要我幫忙找的嗎？」
與上一句非常類似，且更有禮貌

例 "May I help you with that?"
「需要我服務嗎？」
顧客可能正在尋找什麼，藉此問話可以了解客人此刻是否
需要幫忙。

2. During the service
服務過程

例 "I can solve that problem."
「我可以解決這個問題。」
顯示出自己有能力且願意承擔。

例 "I will take responsibility."
「我會負這個責任。」
表示會負責任。

例 "I'll check and be right back."
「我查一下，馬上回來。」
表明雖不知道，但會去詢問，並馬上回覆。

例 "I don't know the answer, but I'll find out."
「我不知道答案，不過我這就去查。」
即使遇到不知道答案時，仍然願意馬上去查詢。

(例) "Will you hold for a moment while I check on that?"

「可不可以請等一下，我這就去查一下？」

請顧客稍等一下，然後快去查答案。

(例) "Just a moment, I will get our specialist X for you."

「請等一下，我請我們的X專家回覆您。」

如果有必要，請專家來解決問題。

(例) "Thanks for waiting."

「謝謝等候。」

此用法可以安撫顧客久候而不耐的情緒。

(例) "I'm sorry, I didn't understand what you said."

「不好意思，我沒有聽懂你說的話。」

先道歉再請對方說明其話語中令人不清楚之處。

3. End of the service
服務結束

(例) "I will keep you updated."

「我會隨時通知您最新消息。」

顧客聽到這樣的話，必定能夠安心離開店家。

例 "I will deliver on time."
「我會準時交貨。」
沒有什麼比聽到會準時交貨更令人放心的了。

例 "It will be just what you ordered."
「我們交的貨會如同您所訂的。」
再度強調所交的貨不會有問題。

例 "The job will be completed on time."
「我們會準時完工的。」
客戶就是想聽這樣的承諾。

例 "We appreciate your business."
「歡迎光顧。」
顧客買完了所需商品後,如果能聽到這一句,就很可能會
再度光臨。

例 "Thank you for shopping with us."
「歡迎光顧本店。」
此用法為上個用法類似,較為口語。

例 "My pleasure!"
「我的榮幸!」
這是當顧客謝謝你的服務時的最佳答案。

② 12 phrases customers do not want to hear
12 個顧客不想聽到的片語

例 "What is wrong?"
「有什麼問題嗎？」
這樣的問法會讓顧客留下不耐煩的感覺。

例 "What's your problem?"
「你有什麼問題？」
這樣聽起來像是質問，會讓人覺得完全都是顧客自己造成的問題。

例 "I think…"
「我想……」
顧客並不想要得到你個人的意見，而是問題的正確解決方式。

例 "To be honest with you,…"
「老實說……」
這樣會使人感到有時你所說的話並不老實，因此會對你的信賴大打折扣。

例 "That's just our policy."
「這就是我們公司的規定。」
這麼回答會給人做事不知變通，不替顧客著想的感覺。

例 "There's nothing I can do."

「我沒有辦法幫上忙。」

顧客會感到你沒有盡力幫忙，你的服務不周全。

例 "That's not my job."

「這不是我份內的工作。」

讓人覺得你在推卸責任，如果真的不是你可以做主的事，要聯絡專門人員。

例 "You'll have to..."

「你必須要……」

避免要顧客 "必須" 做任何事情，客人並不想要有額外的工作或負擔。

例 "Are you confused?"

「你混淆了嗎？」

這樣會讓人留下輕視顧客能力的印象，可以問說是否需要再解說一遍。

例 "Are you happy now?"

「你現在滿意了吧？」

這樣問會給人想要打發顧客的感覺，似乎顧客所要求的已經超出合理範圍。

例 "Are you unsatisfied?"

「你還不滿意嗎？」

這樣問更會使顧客覺得不受歡迎，很難伺候的感覺。

例 "No problem."
「沒問題。」
顧客並不想被視為是個問題，所以最好避免這麼說。

三、情境對話 Situational Conversations 58

1. Looking for a present
尋找禮物

A "Good afternoon. Can I help you find something?"

B "I'm looking for a birthday present for my 8 year-old nephew."

A "How about this children's book?"

B "Is this illustration done by a Taiwanese artist?"

A "Absolutely, the artist has won several international awards for illustration."

B "Please wrap the book in gift paper for me. Thank you."

Ⓐ「午安，有什麼需要我幫忙找的嗎？」

Ⓑ「我在找給我八歲姪子的生日禮物。」

Ⓐ「這一本童書怎麼樣？」

Ⓑ「這插畫是由台灣藝術家畫的嗎？」

Ⓐ「一點也不錯，這位藝術家曾贏得多項國際插畫獎。」

Ⓑ「請幫我將這本書用包裝紙包起來，謝謝。」

---

2. Refund
退錢

Ⓐ "What can I help you with?"

Ⓑ "Recently I bought the jacket, and it just didn't fit. I'd like to ask for a refund."

Ⓐ "Let me check the receipt. You bought the jacket 8 days ago. Do you know we can only give a refund within 7 days?"

Ⓑ "Is there anything you can do?"

Ⓐ "Instead of a refund, you can exchange the jacket with a good of the same price."

Ⓐ「有什麼我可以服務的嗎？」

Ⓑ「最近我買了一件夾克，但是就是不合身，我想要退錢。」

🅐 「讓我看看收據，您是在八天前買了這件夾克。您知道我們只能在七天內退錢嗎？」

🅑 「請幫幫忙好嗎？」

🅐 「雖然不能退錢，但是您能換一件和夾克同價錢的商品。」

3. Warranty service
保固服務

🅐 "Is there anything I can do for you today?"

🅑 "This is the laptop I bought from you in February, and it is now broken."

🅐 "Do you have the warranty card with you?"

🅑 "Of course, here you are."

🅐 "That's great. It is within the warranty period, and we can fix it for you for sure."

🅐 「今天有什麼我可以服務的嗎？」

🅑 「這是我二月時向您買的筆記型電腦，現在壞了。」

🅐 「您有帶保固書嗎？」

🅑 「當然，這就是。」

🅐 「太好了，還在保固期內，我們一定可以為您修復。」

4. Customer service at a call center
呼叫中心的客服

Ⓐ "Thank you for calling the First Real Estate Agency. My name is Mary Huang. How can I help you?"

Ⓑ "I am searching for a rental space in this area. Could you help me with that?"

Ⓐ "May I ask if this is for an office or for private home?"

Ⓑ "It is for my family of 2 adults and 2 small kids."

Ⓐ "Just hold on for a second. I will put you through to our real estate agent, Mr. Li."

Ⓑ "Thank you very much."

Ⓐ 「這裡是第一房地產公司，謝謝您來電，我叫黃瑪莉，有什麼需要我服務的？」

Ⓑ 「我在尋找這地區的租屋，您能幫我這個忙嗎？」

Ⓐ 「請問這是要用來當辦公室還是私人住家呢？」

Ⓑ 「是我們家要住的，我們有兩個大人，兩個小小孩。」

Ⓐ 「請等一下，我為您接通我們的房屋仲介李先生。」

Ⓑ 「非常感謝。」

四、字彙庫 Word Bank

illustration [ɪˌlʌsˈtreʃən] *n.*　插圖

absolutely [ˈæbsəˌlutlɪ] *adv.* 【口】
　　　　　　　　　　　（用於對答）一點不錯，完全對

refund [ˈriˌfʌnd] *n.*　　退款；償還金額

receipt [rɪˈsit] *n.*　　收據

warrenty [ˈwɔrəntɪ] *n.*　保固書；擔保

estate [ɪsˈtet] *n.*　　地產

search [sɝtʃ] v.　　搜尋

rental [ˈrɛnt!] *a.*　　供出租的

specialist [ˈspɛʃəlɪst] *n.*　專家

relocation [riloˈkeʃən] *n.*　改換所在地

掌握語調

　　語調傳遞許多訊息，說話者的態度與情緒，都會由音調、音量，還有說話的速度直接反映出來，因此客服人員必須要能控制得宜，特別是在電話通話中，更不能洩露出快失去耐心的樣子，這樣顧客才不會臨時改變購買意願。

認同客服工作

　　倘若認同客服工作，就會讓人自然而然有耐心對待各類型的顧客，會願意盡力達成各種任務，如果遇到困難也會想方設法去克服；相反的，如果打從內心看輕客服工作，或者根本就不喜歡接觸客人，那麼就算想要裝出一副和善的樣子，還是很容易被人看穿，在遇到問題時，非常可能很快就會放棄。

Collaboration Across Departments

跨部門合作

一、簡介 Short Introduction

MP3 59

　　跨部門合作並非是一件容易的事，因為很多不同的部門經常處於競爭的狀態，導致無法有效率合作；再者，因為所處理的業務類型不同，對彼此的專業可能理解不多，因而對事務難易程度的判斷可能差別頗大，甚至所使用的語彙都略有出入，這些都會造成在請求其它部門支援時的溝通障礙。以下所整理出的相關英語用法實用且常見，請務必勤加練習，讓這些表達方式深植於腦中，變成自己的習慣語法，如此一來，在需要向對方開口求助或要說服人時，自然而然能夠不假思索就脫口而出，乃至於能夠自由變化，發展出個人風格。

二、 常用表達方式 Useful Expressions

1. Finding out their intentions
　　找出對方的意圖

例 Tell me more about it.
　告訴我更多有關的事。

例 Go on.
　繼續說。

例 Tell me what you mean by....
　告訴我你說……的意思。

例 Are you saying that...?

你是說……？

例 Why would you tell me this?

你為什麼要告訴我這個呢？

例 What would you ask me this?

你為什麼要問我這個呢？

例 Let me ask you this...

讓我問你這個問題……

例 Let me clarify this...

讓我澄清這一點……

例 Please give me an example to help me understand this...

請舉個例子來幫我明白這點……

2. Negotiating
協調

例 I understand how you feel, but...

我了解你的感受，不過……

例 I know what it feels like, but...

我明白你的感覺，不過……

例 I agree with you, but you also know that...

我同意你的看法，不過你也明白……

例 I see your point, but what about...?

我明白你要說的重點，不過……該怎麼辦呢？

例 Let me remind you that...
容我提醒你一點……

例 I'm afraid this is against our policy to....
這恐怕不符合我們公司政策……

3. Persuading others
說服他人

例 I think you should...
我認為你應該……

例 I can give you some suggestions to...
我可以給你一些建議……

例 Have you thought about...?
你有沒有想過……？

例 Would that help if I...
如果我……能對此有幫助嗎？

例 What do you think would happen if...
如果我……你想會怎麼樣呢？

例 In cases like that, I would...
像這樣的情形我會……

例 I probably would not...
我可能不會……

4. Asking for support
請求支援

例 Could you send an IT specialist to us to...?
你可不可以派個資訊專家來……？

例 Could you spare a couple of people to help us with...?
你有沒有多兩三個人可以幫我們……？

例 Could you spare an hour to...?
你可不可以撥出一個小時來……？

例 Do you know any suitable technician to...?
你是否認識任何合適的技術人員來……？

例 Do you happen to know any person who can...?
你是否剛好認識可以……的人？

例 Do you have someone available on your team to...?
你們團隊裡是否有人方便能夠……？

5. Responding to requests for support
對支援需求的回覆

例 What would you like us to do for you?
你希望我們幫你們做什麼？

例 Would it help if I...?
如果我……能有幫助嗎？

例 What do you think would happen if I...?
你覺得如果我……會發生什麼事呢？

例 I suggest that we work together to...
我建議我們一起來……

例 I can recommend a good person to...
我可以推薦一個合適的人來……

例 I'll ask around for you...
我可以替你四處打聽一下……

例 As soon as I find someone, I'll let you know.
只要我找到人，就會告訴你。

例 I'm afraid I cannot help you this time.
這次我恐怕無法幫你。

三、情境對話 Situational Conversations 60

(1)

A Could you send an expert to explain to us how to use the new database of our company?

B Could I have someone instruct you on the phone instead of asking a person to come over?

A I'm afraid it is not possible. We urgently need someone to demonstrate to us how the new database works.

Ⓑ I see. May I ask when it would be a good time for you?

Ⓐ As soon as possible.

Ⓑ How about one o'clock tomorrow afternoon?

Ⓐ That will do.

Ⓐ 你可以派一位專家來向我們解釋公司的新資料庫如何使用嗎？

Ⓑ 我可不可以不派人過去，而請人在電話裡教你們嗎？

Ⓐ 恐怕不太可能，我們急著要人為我們示範這新資料庫是如何運作的。

Ⓑ 我明白了。請問什麼時間對你們方便？

Ⓐ 越快越好。

Ⓑ 明天下午一點怎麼樣？

Ⓐ 可以。

(2)

Ⓐ Could you have someone suitable come here to help us install the schedule control software?

Ⓑ At the moment, I cannot provide anyone to support you, since all people on our team are extremely busy.

Ⓐ What a shame. Is there anything you could do for me?

Ⓑ How about you contact the IT company that sold us the software and see if they could help you out?

Ⓐ Do you really think they would give us a hand?

Ⓑ Yes, I'm pretty sure because yesterday they sent us an IT person to install the software after I rang them.

Ⓐ 你可不可以派個合適的人來這裡幫我們安裝進度控制軟體嗎？

Ⓑ 目前我無法提供任何人支援你，因為我們團隊所有人都非常忙。

Ⓐ 真可惜，你有沒有什麼辦法可以幫我的呢？

Ⓑ 你不妨聯絡賣軟體給我們的資訊公司，看看他們是否可以幫你忙？

Ⓐ 你真的認為他們會幫我們忙？

Ⓑ 我非常確定，因為昨天我打電話給他們後，他們就派了一個資訊人員來為我們安裝這個軟體。

(3)

Ⓐ What would you like us to do for you?

Ⓑ Could you have a legal expert help us draw a contract?

Ⓐ It depends on what sort of a contract it is.

Ⓑ It is about copyright.

Ⓐ In that case, I'll recommend Ms. Wang. She'll be with you right away.

Ⓐ 有什麼需要我們服務的呢？

Ⓑ 你能夠請一位法律專家來協助我們擬定一份合約嗎？

Ⓐ 這要看是哪一類的合約。

Ⓑ 是關於著作版權。

Ⓐ 這樣的話，我會推薦王小姐，她馬上會過去你那邊。

(4)

Ⓐ I need some extra hands to prepare for the trade fair!

Ⓑ There is not much I can do about it at all. We are falling behind schedule and cannot support you.

Ⓐ That's too bad.

Ⓑ Have you thought of outsourcing your work to people outside of the company?

Ⓐ That sounds like a great idea. Where would you suggest me to look for suitable candidates?

Ⓑ I can recommend some useful apps to you.

Ⓐ Fantastic.

Ⓐ 我需要人幫忙準備商展！

Ⓑ 我沒有辦法幫上任何的忙，我們的進度落後，無法幫你們。

Ⓐ 真可惜。

Ⓑ 你是否想過將你們的工作外包給公司外的人？

Ⓐ 似乎是個好主意，你會建議我到哪兒尋找合適的人選呢？

Ⓑ 我可以推薦一些有用的應用程式給你。

Ⓐ 太好了。

四、字彙庫 Word Bank

clarify [ˋklærəˌfaɪ] v.	澄清；闡明
persuade [pɚˋswed] v.	說服，勸服
suggestion [səˋdʒɛstʃən] n.	建議，提議
spare [spɛr] v.	分出，騰出（時間，人手）
database [ˋdetəˌbes] n.	資料庫，數據庫
instruct [ɪnˋstrʌkt] v.	教授；訓練；指導
demonstrate [ˋdɛmənˌstret] v.	示範操作，展示
legal [ˋlig!] a.	法律上的，有關法律的
copyright [ˋkɑpɪˌraɪt] n.	版權；著作權
outsource [ˈaʊtsɔːs] v.	將…外包

貼 心 小 叮 嚀

合乎情理

　　就如同人與人之間要求幫忙，不宜有不情之請，請求跨部門合作也需要合乎情理，也就是說要請對方幫忙的性質與工作量要考量到對方的能力，而且還要適時做出回饋，如果平時經常提供協助給別的部門，那麼在自己的部門遇到需要支援時，也就容易得到跨部門的救兵了。除此之外，在溝通過程中，要注意讓彼此都感到自在，沒有受到威脅的感覺，最後才容易達成雙贏。

要判斷最佳時機

　　做任何事情都要掌握時機，尤其是需要別人伸出援手時，更要研判時間點是否合宜，倘若時機不對，例如在別人正是缺乏時間與資金的時候，貿然提出請求支援的要求，那麼即使你的態度與口氣多麼委婉低下，對方極可能也只能表示愛莫能助。

Chapter

18

Hosting a Guest

接待訪客

一、簡介 Short Introduction

 61

　　接待來訪客人看似簡單，但是當中有很多的細節要注意，尤其是接待首次來訪的外國訪客，更需要花心思，才能讓來訪的客人留下對公司的良好印象。本章分為機場、飯店、餐廳的三個常見場景，來探討可能會用到的各種英語表達方式，基本而且實用，只要稍加練習，必定能順利達成目的，熟能生巧。

二、常用表達方式 Useful Expressions

Unit
1.

At the Airport
在機場

1. Welcoming a guest at the airport
接機

例 How was your flight?
你旅途順利嗎？

例 How are you feeling after such a long flight?
經過這麼長途飛行你感覺怎麼樣？

例 Nice to meet you.
很高興認識你。

例 Would you like to exchange money now?
你想要換錢嗎？

例 Let's take a taxi over there.
我們去那邊搭計程車。

例 Please allow me to carry the suitcase for you.
請讓我為您提行李。

例 Let me take your baggage for you.
讓我為你提行李。

例 Would you like to grab something to eat first?
你想要先吃點東西嗎？

例 How about having a cup of coffee together over there?
要不要一起去那邊喝杯咖啡？

例 Is there anything you need to get before taking a bus to the hotel?
在我們搭車去飯店前你需要買些什麼嗎？

2. Seeing off a guest at the airport
送機

例 Which airline are you flying on?
你要搭哪家航空？

例 What is your flight number?
你搭的航班是幾號？

例 When is your flight?

你的班機是在什麼時候？

例 What is your departure time?

你飛機幾點起飛？

例 Is your flight a direct flight or do you have to transfer to another flight?

你的班機是直飛的或是你得專機？

例 How did you like your stay here?

你喜歡待在這裡嗎？

例 I hope you enjoyed your time here.

希望你喜歡待在這裡的時光。

例 Is there anything you need to do before heading home?

在回家前你還有什麼需要做的事嗎？

例 Have you bought all the souvenirs to take home?

你買了所有要帶回家的紀念品嗎？

例 Come back to visit us soon!

快點回來看我們！

在旅館

---

1. Hotel Check-in
旅館入住手續

例 Have you reserved a room in a hotel yet?
你訂了飯店房間了嗎？

例 Which hotel do you prefer to stay in?
你比較喜歡待在哪間飯店？

例 Do you need me to book a hotel for you?
你需要我幫你訂飯店嗎？

例 You'll be staying at the Sheraton Hotel.
你將住在喜來登大飯店。

例 The service of this hotel should be quite decent.
這家飯店的服務應該相當不錯。

例 You will have to show your passport to the staff at the check-in counter.
你要將護照給辦理入住手續的櫃檯人員看。

例 Please check the dates of your reservation carefully.
請仔細檢查你的預約日期。

例 I've reserved a suite at the Sheraton for you for the following 3 days.
我為您訂了喜來登大飯店接下來三天的一間套房。

例 If you like the service at the Sheraton, you can extend your stay there.

如果您喜歡喜來登大飯店的服務，您可以延長住宿時間。

例 We'll have dinner together in the restaurant at the Sheraton tomorrow evening.

我們明天下午會在喜來登大飯店的飯店共進晚餐。

2. Hotel Check-out
旅館退房

例 Did you check your room thoroughly before leaving?

你離開時是否仔細檢查了房間？

例 Have you got all of your things in the room?

你是否帶了房間內你所有的東西？

例 How did you like the service of the hotel?

你喜歡這家飯店的服務嗎？

例 Is the bill accurate?

這份帳單正確嗎？

例 Please take a look at the bill.

請看一看這份帳單。

例 How come you have the extra charges on your bill?

你帳單上怎麼會有額外費用？

例 Do you want me to go through your bill?

你要我幫你檢查帳單嗎？

例 Would you want to take a look at the souvenir shop in the hotel?

你想要看看飯店的紀念品店嗎？

例 Do you want me to call a taxi for you?

你想要我幫你叫輛計程車嗎？

例 There is a cab waiting outside the door of the hotel for us.

飯店門外有輛計程車在等著我們。

Unit
3. In a restaurant   🎵 63

在餐廳

1. 點菜

例 Would you like to have some red wine?

你想要先來些紅酒嗎？

例 How about some Taiwanese beer before the meal?

用餐前先來喝點台灣啤酒好嗎？

例 Is there anything that you don't eat?

是否有哪些食物是你不吃的？

例 Is there anything special you would like to try?

是否有哪些特別的食物是你想要嚐嚐看的？

例 Do you eat spicy food?

你吃不吃辣？

例 Would you like to take a look at the menu?

你是否想看一下菜單？

例 Should I order the dishes for you?

需要為你點餐嗎？

例 Would you like to try Yam Cha or Taiwanese dishes?

你想要試試港式飲茶還是台灣料理？

例 Would you like to order lunch set menu?

你想要點午餐套餐嗎？

例 We'll decide if we should order some desserts afterwards.
我們等一會兒再決定是否需要點一些甜點。

2. 用餐結束

例 How did you like the dishes we just had?
你喜歡我們剛吃的餐點嗎？

例 Was the food here alright with you?
這裡的食物你覺得還可以嗎？

例 Let me take care of the bill.
帳單讓我來負責。

例 The dinner is on me.
晚餐我請客。

例 I insist on treating you this time.
這次我堅持要請你。

例 This is your first meal here, and I'd like to treat you.
這是你在這裡的第一餐，我想要請你。

例 You can take the extra food to the hotel if you want to.
如果你想要的話，可以將多餘的食物打包帶回飯店。

例 Would you like to order another beer?
你想要再點一瓶啤酒嗎？

例 If you have time, we can go together to a café nearby.
如果你有時間的話，我們可以一起到附近的一家咖啡館。

三、情境對話 Situational Conversations

(1)

Ⓐ You must be Mr. Richardson.

Ⓑ Yes, I am. Thank you for coming to the airport to pick me up.

Ⓐ Let me carry your suitcase for you.

Ⓑ Thanks. Are we going to the city directly right now?

Ⓐ Yes, I ordered a taxi to take us straight from the airport to your hotel in the city.

Ⓑ Thank you for being so thoughtful.

Ⓐ 您一定是理查森先生。

Ⓑ 我正是,謝謝來機場接我。

Ⓐ 讓我來替您提行李。

Ⓑ 謝謝,我們現在要直接到市區嗎?

Ⓐ 是的,我已訂了計程車,可以直接將我們從機場載到您在市區的飯店。

Ⓑ 謝謝您如此體貼。

(2)

A I booked a single room in a hotel nearby for you from May 31 to June 3.

B Lovely. What is the hotel called?

A It is called Greenery Hotel, and it is within walking distance to the Taipei train station.

B That suits me very well. You know that I often cannot find my way in a new environment.

A Why don't we walk to the hotel together now so that we can immediately get you check in?

A 我為您在附近的旅館訂了五月 31 日至六月 3 日的單人房。

B 很好，那家旅館叫什麼？

A 叫作綠意旅舍，從台北火車站走路就可以到達。

B 那樣對我很適合，你知道我在新環境常常會迷路。

A 我們何不現在就一起走到那家旅舍，好讓你馬上辦好入住手續？

(3)

A Let's go to the Yam Cha restaurant for dinner in the hotel you are staying in.

B That's great. I haven't had any Chinese food for a long time.

A But I insist the dinner is on me.

B Thank you. That's very kind of you.

A I hope you will like the dishes over there.

A 我們今晚去你住的飯店吃港式飲茶。

B 真是個好主意，我已經很久沒有吃中國料理。

A 但是我堅持晚餐我請客。

B 謝謝，你真是好心。

A 希望你會喜歡那兒的餐點。

四、字彙庫 Word Bank

suitcase [`sutˌkes] *n.*	小型旅行箱；手提箱
baggage [`bægɪdʒ] *n.*	行李
departure [dɪ`partʃɚ] *n.*	出發，起程
transfer [træns`fɚ] *v.*	轉機；轉車
decent [`disnt] *a.*	像樣的；還不錯的
reservation [ˌrɛzɚ`veʃən] *n.*	預訂

suite [swit] *n.*	套房
extend [ɪkˋstɛnd] *v.*	延長，延伸
accurate [ˋækjərɪt] *a.*	準確的；精確的
thoughtful [ˋθɔtfəl] *a.*	體貼的；細心的

注意細節，不斷改進

　　如果能用心做好事前準備，盡心扮演好接待角色，掌握接待流程中的各種細微之處，必定會使訪客感到賓至如歸，並且因為種種體貼的安排而感動。在賓客離去後，也要好好檢討，不斷改進，那麼一定會不斷進步。

保持彈性

　　訪客隨時都可能因為天候或體力等因素而臨時更改行程，因此要彈性處理原定計畫，最好備有多個替代方案，那麼才比較不會臨時手忙腳亂，如果可行的話，先與訪客在事前討論替代方案，並且先徵求同意，這樣才能讓訪客感到受到尊重。

Chapter

(19)

Arranging Travel Plans

安排旅遊計畫

一、簡介 Short Introduction

　　安排旅遊計畫時，事前的準備非常重要，包含食宿與交通工具的安排等，都要與客人商量過，各人的喜好不同，有人偏愛都會生活，有人較愛親近人跡罕至的大自然，因此為訪客安排旅遊計畫時，務必要考量個人的興趣和想要參觀的景點。如果你能夠全程為訪客提供口譯，那當然是最好不過，但是如果你無法陪同客人一起旅遊，就需要儘量安排附有英語服務的民宿與餐廳，在本章中你可以學習到很多關於安排旅行相關細節的英語用法，不妨參考看看，並且運用所學做一些彈性變化。

三、常用表達方式 Useful Expressions 64

1. Discussing the trip
討論旅遊事項

例 Where would you like to go on the weekend?
這周末您想要去哪兒？

例 What would you like to see during your stay here?
您想要在這次停留期間看些什麼？

例 What do you want to experience this time?
您這次想要體驗點什麼？

例 What sort of activities would you be interested in?
什麼樣的活動您會感興趣呢？

例 Do you have anything special in mind that you would like to do here?
您在這兒是否有什麼特別想做的事情嗎？

例 Is there any place special that you would like to visit?
有什麼特別的地方是您想要去參觀的呢？

例 Do you prefer taking public transportation or renting a car?
您比較想要搭乘大眾交通工具或是租車？

例 Would you be interested in learning the indigenous culture?
您對於學習原住民文化是否會感興趣呢？

例 How about going hiking in the Yangming Mountain this coming Sunday?
這星期日去陽明山健行好嗎？

例 Please let us know your preferences so that we can organize your trip.
請讓我們知道您的偏好，這樣我們才好為您安排旅程。

2. Reviewing the trip
回顧旅程

例 Do you like most scenic spots you have been to?
您喜歡大部分你去過的景點嗎？

例 How was your impression of this country overall?

您對這個國家整體的印象如何？

例 What was your favorite place of your trip?

這趟旅程中您最喜歡哪一部分？

例 What were the highlights of your travel?

這趟旅行對您來說哪一部分最精彩？

例 What stands out in your travel experiences?

這趟旅行中有什麼對您是很特別的經驗嗎？

例 Where would you recommend your friends to travel here?

您會建議您的朋友來這兒旅遊嗎？

例 Is there any place you would like to definitely visit again?

有什麼地方讓您覺得一定要再去一趟嗎？

例 What do you think of the arrangements of accommodation and food?

您覺得住宿與餐飲的安排如何？

例 What would you like us to improve upon next time?

有什麼是您想要我們下次改進的？

例 It is our pleasure to arrange the trips during your stay here.

能為您在這裡的停留期間安排旅行事項是我們的榮幸。

四、情境對話 Situational Conversations 65

(1)

A Do you know any place nearby for me to get away from the city to enjoy the nature for a while?

B Sure. I'd recommend Maokong if you feel like enjoying the fresh air and the greenery on the mountain.

A Is it easy to get there?

B Yes, you can first take the MRT to the Taipei Zoo and then take the Maokong Gondola to Maokong.

A That sounds like fun.

B When you arrive in Maokong, you will find there are plenty of tea restaurants to choose from.

A That must be an ideal place for afternoon tea.

A 你知道附近有什麼地方可以讓我暫時離開都市,享受一下大自然?

B 當然有的,如果你想要享受山上的新鮮空氣與綠色植物,我會推薦貓空。

A 到那邊的交通方便嗎?

Ⓑ 很方便，你可以先搭捷運到台北動物園，然後搭乘貓纜到貓空。

Ⓐ 聽起來挺好玩的。

Ⓑ 當你到達貓空，你會發現有很多的茶餐廳供你挑選。

Ⓐ 想必那一定是下午茶的理想地方。

(2)

Ⓐ I'd like to take my family to visit the Taroko Gorge during this long weekend. Could you help me arrange that?

Ⓑ I happen to know a nice bed and breakfast over there, and I can call and reserve the rooms for you in a second.

Ⓐ That's great. My parents will join my family to travel down there, and that means we need altogether 2 double rooms.

Ⓑ All right. Last time I stayed there with my friends, they offered us tasty indigenous dishes for dinner. Would you like me to book that for you as well?

Ⓐ Of course, who can resist delicious local cuisines in a trip?

Ⓑ One more thing, it's not easy to get the train tickets for holidays because so many people are trying to buy the tickets at the same time.

Ⓐ In that case, please arrange a taxi for us, and I'll pay for the all expenses of the taxi driver to travel with us.

Ⓐ 我想要帶我的家人在這個周末連休去太魯閣峽谷去玩，你能幫我安排嗎？

Ⓑ 我碰巧知道一家很好的民宿，我馬上可以打電話為你訂房。

Ⓐ 太好了，我父母親會和我家人一同前往那兒，也就是說我們總共需要兩間雙人房。

Ⓑ 好的。上次我和朋友待在那裡，他們提供了美味的原住民餐點給我們當晚餐，你也要我為你們訂餐嗎？

Ⓐ 當然，有誰能夠在旅行中抗拒得了當地美食呢？

Ⓑ 還有一件事，假日的火車票一票難求，因為很多人都要在同時間內試著買到票。

Ⓐ 那麼請為我安排計程車，我會負擔計程車司機與我們一同旅遊的全部費用。

(3)

Ⓐ Now you are about to fly back to your country. What is your most memorable travel experience in Taiwan?

Ⓑ If I have to name one, it must be the trip to Taitung.

Ⓐ What makes you think so?

Ⓑ There seems to be something special about that place. I felt that I could completely unwind when I was in the countryside there.

Ⓐ Please come back to Taiwan soon and have a good time in the beautiful scenery.

Ⓐ 現在你就要搭飛回國了,你在台灣最值得回味的旅遊經驗為何?

Ⓑ 如果一定要說出一個,那必定非台東之旅莫屬。

Ⓐ 你為什麼會這樣認為呢?

Ⓑ 那裡似乎就是有什麼特別之處,在那邊的鄉下我感覺能夠完全放鬆。

Ⓐ 請早日再回來台灣享受美好風景。

四、字彙庫 Word Bank

indigenous [ɪnˋdɪdʒɪnəs] a.		原住民的；本地的
preference [ˋprɛfərəns] n.		偏愛
highlight [ˋhaɪ͵laɪt] n.		最精彩的部分
recommend [͵rɛkəˋmɛnd] v.		推薦，介紹
definitely [ˋdɛfənɪtlɪ] adv.		肯定地；當然
arrangement [əˋrendʒmənt] n.		安排；準備工作
accommodation [ə͵kɑməˋdeʃən] n.	住處
gorge [gɔrdʒ] n.		峽谷
resist [rɪˋzɪst] v.		抗拒
cuisine [kwɪˋzin] n.		菜餚

貼心安排旅程

　　有些初次到來的訪客對於想參觀的景點沒有做任何功課，因此可能得要完全仰賴你的安排，這時你可以先幫他們收集旅遊資料，甚至買一本旅遊書送給他們，然後詢問他們可能會感興趣的風景與活動。有時你無法全程陪你的訪客，還有些時候，訪客比較想要享受與家人獨處的時光，這時就要靠你事先就將食宿與交通等事項安排妥當，你的訪客一定會對你非常感激，因為你幫上了他們一個大忙。

打點旅遊細節不馬虎

　　有些商務旅客的主要目的不在觀光，因此可以供旅遊的時間可能極為有限，說不定只有三至四天可以安排，但是卻提出想要環島的要求，加上大部分人不通中文，因此要為他們打點好大大小小的旅遊相關事項，真的不是一件容易的事。除了一般要注意的事項，例如避免一再更改預定日期、人數等等，以免造成業主的混淆，還要特別提醒客人個人的特殊細節，例如飲食、飲酒的禁忌、謝絕購物行程等。

Chapter

(20)

Annual Self-Evaluation
年度自我評量

一、 簡介 Short Introduction

　　年度自我評量是公司每年提供給員工對自己一年來表現的評論,好讓主管可以從員工的角度看一年的進展,通常會要員工反省一年來的成就與失敗事項,重點常會放在是否達成自己所預設的目標,完成了哪些主管交代的任務,是否有傑出的個人與團隊表現,或是否有哪些有待改善的地方。在員工完成年度自我評量之後,主管會依此表達是否贊同的意見,通常人事部門只會讓員工知道他們的主管對其年度自我評量的意見,而不會告知他們的同事相關事項。

二、常用表達方式 Useful Expressions

 66

Unit
1. Discussing the annual self-evaluation

討論年度自我評量

How would rate your own performance in the last year? Not so good/average/good/excellent? Why?
你對自己去年的表現會如何評分?不太好/普通/好/很好?為什麼?

Answer

☞ I would say excellent because I successfully accomplished all my projects.

我會說很好，因為我成功地完成了我所有的專案。

Answer

☞ Last year was a good year to me, since all my clients were pleased with my service.

去年對我來說是個好年，因為所有我的客戶都對我的服務感到滿意。

Question 2.

☞ Have you achieved most of your goals within the past 12 months?

過去十二個月中，你是否達成你大部分的目標？

Answer

☞ Yes, not only do I reach the objectives, but I have also managed time well.

是的，我不但達成了目標，而且我也將時間管理得很好。

Answer

☞ No, but I'll finish them very soon.

並沒有，但是我很快就會完成。

Question 3.

What were the most difficult challenges you encountered last year?

去年當中你遇到的最大挑戰有哪些？

Answer

☞ Making each one on our team contribute to the joint project.

讓我們團隊的每個人都對共同的專案做出貢獻。

Answer

☞ I would say fund raising and risk management.

我會說是募資與危機管理。

Question 4.

What would you like to improve upon in the following year?

什麼是你明年當中最想要改善的？

Answer

☞ Above all, my leadership.

特別是我的領導能力。

Answer

☞ I would like to work on my English and computer skills.

我想要在英文和電腦技能方面下功夫。

Question 5.

What would you like your supervisor to do to improve your performance in your current position?

你希望你的主管如何幫助你，以改善你在目前職位上的表現？

Answer

☞ Not assigning tasks at the last minute.

不要在最後一分鐘才分派工作。

Answer

☞ I would like to have online English lessons paid by the company.

我希望公司能為我付網路英文課程的費用。

Question 6.

What do you consider to be your greatest achievements in the past year?

你認為你在去年當中最大的成就為何？

Answer

☞ My sales record was the highest compared to others last year.

在去年當中我的銷售業績比其他人都高。

Answer

☞ During last year, I managed to stay focused and calm most of the time while doing customer service.
在去年當中，我在做客服的時候，大都能保持專注且冷靜。

Question 7.

What are the goals you set for yourself in the coming year?
在未來的一年中你給自己定下了什麼目標？

Answer

☞ Time management and work-life balance.
時間管理以及工作與生活之間的平衡。

Answer

☞ Within next year, I would very much like to finish this project at hand.
在明年內我非常想要完成手上的這個專案。

Unit 2. Reviewing last year

MP3 67

回顧去年

Question 1.

List the goals you set out to achieve in the last year, and write your own comments on your performance as self-appraisal.

列出你在去年當中想要達成的目標，寫下你對自己表現的意見以作為自我評量。

Answer

☞ I set out to accomplish 3 major projects within last year, and I finished them all. I was pleased with myself.

在去年當中我預計要完成三項主要的專案，我都完成了。我對自己感到滿意。

Answer

☞ During the past year, I made good use of the online English courses paid by the company, and now I can give a presentation in English.

在去年當中，我善加利用公司付費的網路英語課程，現在我能夠做英文簡報。

Unit

3. **Planning next year** 🎵 68

計畫未來的一年

Question 1.

List the objectives for the next year. What training workshops or courses would you like to attend to develop those skills to achieve your aims?

列出明年的目標，你有沒有什麼要參加的培訓工作坊或是課程，以培養這些技能來達成目標？

Answer

☞ I'd like to learn Japanese in order to improve the communication with my clients from Tokyo. Is there sponsorship the company could provide?

我想要學日文好讓我改善與東京來的客戶的溝通，不知道公司是否能提供贊助？

Answer

☞ As a new manager, I've felt the need to learn more about being a leader, and I was wondering if there were any training programs in the company?

身為新經理，我深感加強學習當領導人的重要性，不知道公司是否有任何的培訓計畫？

三、情境對話 Situational Conversations

(1)

A What do you consider to be your greatest achievements in the past year?

B Thanks to the English training courses provided by the company, I successfully hosted our American boss in Taiwan all by myself.

A I heard you also organized a trip to the Sun Moon Lake for the boss after the plant tour.

B Yes, and he seemed to be very pleased with everything.

A The boss was so impressed with your arrangements and guide that he said he would visit Taiwan next year as well.

B I am glad to hear that.

A And we are proud of you.

A 你自認為在去年當中最大的成就為何？

B 因為有公司提供的英語訓練課程，我獨自成功完成了在台灣接待美國老闆的任務。

A 我聽說你也為老闆在參觀工廠後，安排了日月潭之旅。

🅑 是的，而且他似乎對一切都很滿意。

🅐 老闆對你的安排與導覽留下了如此深刻的印象，他説明年他還要再來台灣參觀。

🅑 聽到這一點，我很高興。

🅐 我們以你為榮。

(2)

🅐 What would you like your supervisor to do to improve your performance?

🅑 He promised to give me a raise if I could reach the sales target, but it never happened.

🅐 Have you talked to him about it?

🅑 Yes, but he told me that it was not a good time.

🅐 Did you ask him why?

🅑 Yes. He replied that the company was not doing well financially.

🅐 All right. I'll talk about it with him if I have the chance.

🅐 你希望你的主管如何幫助你，以改善你的表現？

🅑 他答應説如果我能達到銷售目標，就會幫我加薪，但是從來沒有。

🅐 你與他談過這個嗎？

🅑 談過，但是他說不是時候。

🅐 你問過他原因嗎？

🅑 問過，他說公司那時財務運轉欠佳。

🅐 好的，如果有機會我會跟他談談。

(3)

🅐 What were some difficulties you had in the last year?

🅑 Many writers revised their contents at the last minute, and I had to redo the layouts as a result several times.

🅐 Did you manage to finish all of them in time?

🅑 Yes, but I think it is not fair because it was not my fault.

🅐 What would you like me to do for you?

🅑 First of all, our editors should ask writers not to fall behind on the deadlines.

🅐 That makes perfect sense.

🅐 在去年當中你遇到了哪些困難呢？

🅑 很多作者在最後一刻變更了內容，導致我好幾次必須要重新排版。

A 你是否都及時完工了？

B 是的，不過我認為這樣對我不公平，因為這並非是我造成的問題。

A 你希望我如何幫你呢？

B 最重要的一點，我們的編輯應該要求作者不可在截稿日期後才交稿。

A 真有道理。

(4)

A What would you like to see done with the Human Resources?

B In the past year, the announcements of the holidays were really confusing, especially with the official make-up working days.

A Could you give an example?

B For example, on Sat, June 4th all workers had to work to make up for the Dragon Boat Festival Holidays, but we didn't have to because our clients did not work on Saturday. The problem was that the announcement came so late that many employees could not arrange their holidays properly.

A I see your point. We will take it into consideration from now on.

B That could help us tremendously.

A 你希望人事部做哪些改變？

B 在去年當中，假日的宣布非常令人困擾，特別是國定的補班日期。

A 可以舉例說明嗎？

B 例如在六月四日星期六所有的勞工需要為端午假期而補班，但是我們不需要，因為我們的客戶在星期六不工作，問題是太晚宣布，導致很多員工無法好好安排假期。

A 我明白你的意思了，從今以後我們會將此納入考量。

B 那樣對我們會有很大的幫助。

四、字彙庫 Word Bank

self-evaluation	自我評價
rate [ret] v.	對……評價
accomplish [əˋkɑmplɪʃ] v.	完成，實現，達到
achieve [əˋtʃiv] v.	完成，實現
goal [gol] n.	目的，目標

objective [əbˋdʒɛktɪv] *n.*	目的，目標
challenge [ˋtʃælɪndʒ] *n.*	挑戰
contribute [kənˋtrɪbjut] *v.*	貢獻
self-appraisal	自我評價
aim [em] *n.*	目的，目標
tremendously [trɪˋmɛndəslɪ] *adv.*	極大地；非常

貼 心 小 叮 嚀

用正面的詞語

　　在做自我評量時，要儘量用正面的方式來呈現自己，例如先陳述優點，然後表示雖然有尚待加強之處，但是非常願意謙虛學習，即便是在描述自己的缺點，也要慎選用詞，不要給人留下太負面的印象。

做好充分的準備

　　年度自我評量可能會牽涉到某些有爭議性的事件，若要向人事部投訴主管或同事，請先準備好收集妥當的證據，包含人證與物證，並撰寫好投訴信，然後沙盤推演，設想可能的最壞結果，例如被降職或辭職，做好萬全的考量再進行。

附
錄

①

Letter of Application
求職信

一、求職信簡介

　　求職信是獲得理想工作的跳板，也可說是進入職場的墊腳石，代表應徵者給人書面上的第一印象，因此在面試的篩選過程扮演著舉足輕重的角色。

二、求職信的寫作要領

🎧 **69**

1. 敬稱
Salutation

通常用敬稱的**Dear**開頭，結尾附上逗號。

🔘 Dear Mr. Abc,
請儘量找出收信人的性名與稱謂。

🔘 Dear Ms. Abc,
現在無論已婚或未婚女性都偏好Ms.的稱謂，但是如果對方有指定想要別人使用的稱謂，如Mrs. 或Miss，則要依照使用用。

🔘 Dear Director (主任),
Dear Project Managers (專案經理),
如果找不到收信人的確切名字，則可以用職位名稱來稱呼，可以是單數也可以是複數的。

例 To whom it concerns,

To whom it may concern,

如果不太清楚是哪一個部門，則可以用相關人員來概稱。

---

2. 主旨：說明應徵項目
Purpose: Position Applied for

例 I'm writing to apply for the position of...
我寫這封信想要申請……

例 I would like to apply for the position of..
我想要申請……

例 In reply to your advertisement...
關於您登的廣告……

例 Regarding the position advertised...
關於您廣告登的職缺……

例 I'd like to inquire about the job vacancy...
我想要詢問關於此職缺相關事項……

3. 爲何應徵（現在與過去工作經驗）
Reasons for Applying

例 In my current work, I am not able to...
我在目前的工作無法……

例 My former boss was not very kind...
我之前的老闆人不太好……

例 I look for a more challenging position...
我期待有更具挑戰性的工作……

例 You have the best talents in your team...
您的團隊有最佳的人才……

例 I'd like to expand my knowledge in this area...
我想要擴展我在這個領域的知識……

例 I can offer you the best skills in this field...
我能提供您在這個領域的最佳技術……

4. 結語
Conclusion

例 I believe I am the right candidate for the position.
我相信我正是最適合這個職缺的人。

例 From my resume, you can see I am very qualified for the position.
從我的履歷表您可以看出我是這個職缺的最適合人選。

例 Please feel free to contact me if you have any questions.
如果您有任何問題，歡迎隨時聯絡我。

例 I look forward to the opportunity of an interview.
我很期待能有面試機會。

例 Thank you for your help.
謝謝您的協助。

5. 頌候語
Closures

Yours sincerely,

Sincerely yours,

Sincerely,

Yours truly,

Best wishes,

Best,

Best regards,

Regards,

三、求職信範例 70

(1) 求職信 範例一（社會新鮮人）& 中譯

Dear Ms. Anderson,

In reply to your advertisement in the Liberty Times, I would like to submit my application for the position of the English news anchor in your TV news station.

It has always been my career goals to work in the field of mass media, and that is why I chose to study in the Department of Journalism & Communication Studies at the Fu Jen Catholic University. During my undergraduate studies, I received solid training in both theories and practices of Journalism, including TV news reporting. In my last summer vacation, I volunteered for an internship in the department of English News for two months in the ICRT radio station.

My outstanding English proficiency is reflected in the excellent score of the TOEIC test. Moreover, in my sophomore year, I was an exchange student in the University of Washington in Seattle for a year and successfully completed all my courses in English with distinction.

Please find the attached English resume and consider an interview at your convenience.

Thank you very much.

Best regards,
Amy Wang

中文翻譯

安德森女士 您好：

我想要申請您於自由時報上所刊登的電視新聞台英語主播一職。

在大眾傳播領域服務一向是我的事業目標，正因為如此，我選擇就讀輔仁大學的新聞傳播學系，在大學期間，我受到新聞學理論與實務的紮實訓練，包含電視新聞報導。在大學最後一個暑假，我毛遂自薦，於廣播電台ICRT 英語新聞部擔任了兩個月的實習生。

我傑出的英語能力可以由多益測驗成績反映出來，除此之外，在大學第二年，我到西雅圖大學當了一年交換學生，成功用英文修畢所有課程且獲得傑出成績。

請見附件中的英文履歷表，並且考慮於您方便時間安排一個面試。

非常感謝。

王艾美 敬上

(2) 求職信 範例二（有工作經驗的社會人士）**& 中譯**

Dear Human Resource Director,

I am writing to apply for the position you advertised in the Taipei Times recently.

As you can see from my resume, I am quite experienced in this area. Currently I am working in the sales department in an American company, and last year my sales performance was the best in the Taiwanese branch office.

From 2009 to 2015, I worked as a sales manager in the IT industry and successfully trained and led a sales team of 78 young people from various backgrounds. I firmly believe I can apply my experiences and know-hows to the work in your company.

I look forward to the opportunity of an interview to talk more about the details. Please feel free to contact me any time if you have any questions. Thank you for your time and your assistance.

Yours sincerely,
Kevin Chen

中文翻譯

人事部主任 您好：

我寫這封信是想要申請您在台北時報上刊登的職缺。
如同您在我的履歷表上所見，我這方面非常有經驗。目前我在一家美商的銷售部門服務，去年我的銷售業績是台灣分公司最優良的。

從2009年至2015年我在資訊科技產業擔任業務經理，成功訓練並領導了由78位由不同背景的年輕人組成的業務團隊。我深信能夠將我的經驗與知識運用到貴公司的工作上。

我希望能夠獲得面試機會來談更多的細節，如果您有任何問題，歡迎隨時聯絡我，感謝您寶貴的時間與協助。

陳凱文 謹上

附

錄

②

Resume

履歷表

一、履歷表簡介

履歷表英文為 Resume （美式英文）或 CV（英式英文），亦即 Curriculum Vitae。

二、 履歷表類型

主要分為以下三大類型：

(1) 時間順序型履歷表 Chronological Resume & 範例

顧名思義，時間順序型履歷表是按照時間順序來撰寫，要注意的是，距今較近的要列於上方，距今較遠的則在下方，請見範例如下：

Amy Wang

Address: 6F, No 1, ZhongHua Rd. Taipei

Phone No: 0911 119 009

E-mail: amywang@yahoo.com.tw

Job objective:

Formosa English News TV anchor

Education:

2016 Graduated with B.A. from the Department of Journalism & Communication Studies at the Fu Jen Catholic University.

2013-2014 Exchange student at the University of Washington, Seattle

2012-2016 Studying in the Department of Journalism & Communication Studies at the Fu Jen Catholic University.

2012 Graduated from New Taipei Municipal Banqiao Senior High School

2009 Graduated from Taipei Municipal Dun Hua Junior High School

Employment:

July & August, 2015, Internship at ICRT English News

Skills (Certificates)

TOEIC 700

Word R1

PowerPoint P1

Campus Activities:
Member of Public Speaking Club

中文翻譯

王艾美

地址：台北市中華路1號6樓
電話號碼：0911 119 009
電子郵件：amywang@yahoo.com.tw

應徵工作項目：
民視英語新聞電視主播

教育：
2016年　　　輔仁大學新聞傳播學系學士
2013-2014年　西雅圖華盛頓大學交換學生
2012-2016年　就讀於輔仁大學新聞傳播學系
2012年　　　畢業於新北市立板橋高級中學
2009年　　　畢業於台北市立敦化國中

工作經驗：
2015年七、八月　ICRT英語新聞部實習生

技能（證照）：
多益 700
Word R1
PowerPoint P1

社團活動：
大眾演說社團團員

(2) 功能型履歷表 Functional Resume & 範例

　　此類表格是針對工作職務需求將技能整理好，以節省雇主篩選時間。

Kevin Chen

Address: 7F, No 1, DaTong Rd. Taichung
TEL: (04) 2233 5566
E-Mail: kevinchen@gmail.com

Objective:
Customer service clerk

Summary of Qualifications:

- Computer
 Chinese Typing: 70 words/min
 English Typing: 80 words/min
 Word R2
 Excel X2

- Languages
 Chinese: Native
 Taiwanese: Native
 English: Fluent
 Japanese: Intermediate

- Customer service
 Customer service clerk at "Taiwan Mobile Co., Ltd."
 Cashier at the front desk of the Eslite Bookstore

Education:

- B.A. from Yu Da University of Science of Technology
- 6 months of English courses at the Language Training & Testing Center

中文翻譯

陳凱文

地址：台中市大同路1號7樓
電話：(04) 2233 5566
電子郵件：kevinchen@gmail.com

應徵項目：
客服人員

專長摘要：

- 電腦
中文打字 每分70字
英文打字 每分80字
Word R2
Excel X2

- 語言
中文：母語
台語：母語
英語：流利
日語：中級

- 客服經驗
於台灣大哥大股份有限公司擔任客服
於誠品書局擔任櫃台收銀員

教育背景：
- 育達商業科技大學學士
- 語言訓練測驗中心六個月英語課程

(3) **Combination Resume** 複合型履歷 **&** 範例

複合型履歷結合前兩種履歷，提供雇主相關訊息，也適度依時間排序。

James Liu

Objective:

Architect for the Main Library of Tamkang University

Personal Data:

Address: No. 68, SanYi Rd, Sanchong District, New Taipei City

TEL: 0934 456 677

E-Mail: jamesliu@gmail.com

Date of Birth: 30 March, 1978

Education:

1997 - 2001 Department of Architecture, Tamkang University

1994 - 1997 Datung High School

Work Experience:

Full-time work:

2008 - 2016 Architect in the Jones Architects

2002 - 2008 Architect in the Dr. Green Architects

2001 - 2002 Internship in the M&K Architects

Voluntary work:

2001 Urban Designer for the DaDaocheng Community

Related Experiences:

2002 till now Articles appeared in the "Taiwan Architect Magazine"

2001 Award of the Youth Interior Designer of the Year

中文翻譯

劉建士

應徵項目：
淡江大學總圖書館之建築師

個人資料：

地址：新北市三重區三義路68號
電話：0934 456 677
電子郵件：jamesliu@gmail.com

生日：1978年三月30日

教育背景：
1997－2001年　淡江大學建築系
1994－1997年　大同高級中學

工作經驗：

全職：
2008－2016 年於瓊斯建築師事務所擔任建築師
2002－2008 年於綠博士建築事務所擔任建築師
2001－2002 年於M&K建築師事務所實習

志工：
2001 年於大稻埕社區擔任都市規劃師

相關經驗：

2002 年至今 文章陸續刊登於台灣《建築師雜誌》
2001 年 獲頒年度青年室內設計師獎

三、總結

　　無論是以上何種履歷表都各有利弊，一般來說，時間順序型履歷表較適合學經歷沒有任何間斷的求職者，例如剛畢業的社會新鮮人；功能型履歷表較適合擁有多項技能，而又想強調特定才能的人；複合型履歷表則於凸顯申請職務所需技能外，亦兼顧職涯的時間先後順序。要注意的是，只要是提及時間的排序，一律是越靠近現在的列於越上方，以方便閱讀者快速搜尋到所需的最新資訊。總而言之，如果能時時都站在讀者的立場來寫履歷表，那麼就必定能掌握到關鍵重點。

Autobiography

自傳

一、自傳簡介

　　寫自傳的要點為專注於與工作相關的事項，避免提及無關的細節，通常是按照時間先後來陳述與應徵相關的有利條件。請參考以下的範例，並加以自由變化：

二、自傳範例 & 中譯

 72

範本

My name is Mary Li. I was born on March 8, 1980 in Taipei and have been living in the city since then. Since I was small, I have developed a deep interest in the field of medicine, and that motivated me later to become a medical student.

During my internship in the Taipei Veterans General Hospital, I was able to have a close observation of the breast cancer patients, who were undergoing treatments. Afterwards, I successfully completed my graduate school in medicine. Upon finishing my graduate studies, I firmly believed that I would want to contribute what I have learned to finding cures for breast cancer.

Please consider seriously my application to work in the Department of General Surgery in your hospital because I am the most suitable candidate you are looking for.

中文翻譯

我的名字叫李瑪麗，我於 1980 年三月八日出生於台北市，之後就一直在這個城市生活。從小我就發展出對醫學方面強烈的興趣，趨使我後來成為了醫學生。

在於台北榮民總醫院實習期間，我得以近距離觀察接受治療的乳癌病患，之後，我成功修畢醫學研究所，完成研究所課程那時，我確信要將所學貢獻於研發乳癌治療方法上。

請認真考慮我向貴院一般外科部門提出的工作應徵，因為我正是您在尋找的最適合人選。

職場英文王：會話能力進階手冊

雅致風靡　典藏文化

親愛的顧客您好，感謝您購買這本書。

為了提供您更好的服務品質，煩請填寫下列回函資料，您的支持是我們最大的動力。

您可以選擇傳真、掃描或用本公司準備的免郵回函寄回，謝謝。

剪下後傳真、掃描或寄回至「221○3新北市汐止區大同路3段194號9樓之1雅典文化收」

姓名：	性別：　□男　　□女
出生日期：　年　　月　　日	電話：
學歷：	職業：　□男　　□女
E-mail：	

地址：□□□

從何得知本書消息：□逛書店 □朋友推薦 □DM廣告 □網路雜誌

購買本書動機：□封面 □書名 □排版 □內容 □價格便宜

你對本書的意見：
內容：□滿意□尚可□待改進　　編輯：□滿意□尚可□待改進
封面：□滿意□尚可□待改進　　定價：□滿意□尚可□待改進

其他建議：

總經銷：永續圖書有限公司

永續圖書線上購物網
www.foreverbooks.com.tw

您可以使用以下方式將回函寄回。

您的回覆，是我們進步的最大動力，謝謝。

① 使用本公司準備的免郵回函寄回。

② 傳真電話：（02）8647-3660

③ 掃描圖檔寄到電子信箱：

　　yungjiuh@ms45.hinet.net

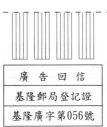

廣　告　回　信
基隆郵局登記證
基隆廣字第056號

2 2 1 0 3

雅典文化事業有限公司　收
新北市汐止區大同路三段194號9樓之1

雅致風靡　典藏文化